Scarecrow on the Marsh

A Cape Cod Thriller

Don Weeks
With
Jonathan Weeks

Scarecrow on the Marsh: A Cape Cod Thriller

Copyright © 2016 by Jonathan Weeks

ISBN 13: 9780998071701

Library of Congress Control Number: 2016952604

Cover design by All Things That Matter Press

Published in 2016 by All Things That Matter Press

To My Father—the best friend I have ever had and the greatest Dad anyone could ask for. You will always be my hero.

Foreword

This book was a labor of love for my father. We vacationed on Cape Cod almost every summer when I was a kid. I can still remember fighting for a window seat as my three sisters and I squeezed into the back of a mid-sized sedan designed to comfortably accommodate only two. One year, we brought our dog along and he slobbered all over us the whole way. There was no air conditioning in the car and tempers would flare on and off for over three hours until we finally spotted the Sagamore Bridge, which signaled our arrival to the Cape. My father delighted in teaching us about every aspect of the place. The lighthouses, beaches, and restaurants—he was intimately familiar with most of them. He knew shortcuts that were kept secret by the native population.

I can vividly recall long walks along the shoreline. My father was never in any hurry to get back to our point of origin. On the contrary, I believe he would have traversed the entire length of the Cape if my sisters and I hadn't complained of being tired or in need of liquid refreshment. He walked with long, purposeful strides and often didn't realize we had fallen behind him until he paused to point out items of interest on the sand, water or skyline. Almost everything I know about the ocean I learned from him.

I remember clearly when my father first got the idea to write a novel. It was in the summer of 1979. I can still picture him sitting at a picnic table in our backyard drinking Narragansett beer, in moderation of course, and scribbling his imaginings onto yellow legal paper. He never used a typewriter. He described himself as "a two-finger typist" and insisted that his thoughts flowed more smoothly when he wrote them down the old-fashioned way. I always loved his handwriting, though it was hard to decipher with all the curlicues and fancy tails on the lower case letters. His chapters were dramatically labeled in a script that resembled wall graffiti. My father was extremely enthusiastic about the creative process. Whenever he felt he had composed a particularly brilliant passage, he would read it aloud to me in a theatrical voice. I listened with rapt attention as he fed me the storyline a page or two at a time. I looked forward to reading it in its entirety but never got the chance. He was about halfway finished with the book when his job began to demand more and more of his time.

After working as a disc jockey, illustrator, TV weatherman, and advertising executive, my father returned to his radio roots in 1980. For three decades, he was WGY's morning show host. He became immensely popular among Capital District listeners, many of whom affectionately referred to him as "Uncle Don." He took great pride in his show, spending long hours at home prepping for it every weekday. His hard work and dedication were officially recognized in 2005 when the National Association of Broadcasters honored him with a Marconi Award. Four years later, he was inducted into the New York State Broadcasters Association Hall of Fame.

At some point during the latter part of his career, I seem to have erased the specific point in time from my memory, my father contracted a rare autoimmune disease known as Wegener's Granulomatosis. It wreaked havoc on him for years, ultimately robbing him of the peaceful retirement he had looked forward to. Though he was sick a great deal of the time, there were extended periods in which the disease was in remission. It was during one of these phases that I suggested he finish the book he had started so many years ago. Despite all his success, my father was always a little unsure of himself. It took a fair amount of persuasion on my part to convince him that the project was worth completing. In the end, he agreed. When he finally got around to working on it, he encountered a major setback:

The old manuscript had been lost along with all the notes.

And so he started over. His zest for writing had not faded a bit. During our weekly phone conversations, which lasted hours sometimes, he tried very hard to leak the entire plot. "No, Dad," I kept telling him. "I want to be surprised when I read it."

"I'll only read you a little bit," he would insist. "Don't worry. I won't give anything away."

By the time I got my hands on a rough draft, a number of traumatic events had taken place. My mother had passed away unexpectedly after falling seriously ill with a brain disorder. My father had been diagnosed with Merkle Cell Cancer—a complication of Wegener's. His daily routine consisted almost entirely of exhausting rounds of dialysis, chemotherapy, and radiation. He fought bravely against the spread of the disease but ultimately lost.

As he lay on his deathbed, I asked my father if he wanted me to try to publish his manuscript after he was gone. He answered "yes" without hesitation and, for a few fleeting seconds, he looked more alive than I had seen him in quite a while. Anyone who has ever met my father knows that his sense of self-worth was derived almost entirely from entertaining people. I'm sure he would have liked nothing more than to connect with his readers and hear what they had to say about the characters and situations he created.

And so here it is—adapted from the original manuscript, which was entirely handwritten. During the editing process, strenuous attempts were made to preserve the integrity of his work. Though I was forced to make extensive alterations, the original story remains virtually intact. I deeply regret the fact that our only collaboration was posthumous. For years, we had talked about engaging in a creative project together but somehow it just never came to be. I hope that this novel brings you as much joy as it did him. He wouldn't have wanted it any other way. He mentioned numerous times that he hoped people would take his book to the beach with them. I'm sure he would be happy to know it was being read by anyone in any setting.

~ Jonathan Weeks

Night of the Scarecrow

1

The boneyard wind.

He forgot when he started calling it that. Something he heard as a child, perhaps.

It blew out of dark and forlorn places. It crept down alleys, rattling windows and moaning around corners. It whispered of sorrow and regret as it sighed its way through the barren branches of leafless trees. Give into it and it would drag you down into an abyss of unbearable torment. It had visited him many times since the double funeral in California and never failed to awaken memories of the terrible losses he had endured.

He tried to focus on the road ahead. The green of summer had given way to autumn's yellows, oranges, and reds. A sudden gust lifted a palette of color and carried leaves away in a swirling cloud that rattled across Route 6A briefly obscuring the headlights of Police Chief Thom Burroughs' black Grand Cherokee.

Burroughs rubbed the highway fatigue from eyes and looked at the dashboard clock. It was almost 11:30 p.m. Most of the Cape's restaurants were either closed for the night or shuttered for the season.

He was hungry.

He had left a police conference in Springfield without staying for the scheduled farewell dinner. He had hoped to grab a quick bite at the Laughing Gull Pub in Dennis before turning in early. A massive backup on the Mass Pike had altered those plans. Two tractor trailers had sideswiped each other and jackknifed across the lanes heading out of Auburn. Traffic had been backed up for miles.

Expelling a heavy sigh, Burroughs decided he had little choice but to settle for a grilled cheese sandwich and a Sam Adams lager at home. Another gust rocked the Jeep. The wind had picked up and was howling through the trees. Their swaying branches were silhouetted against the slate gray sky.

Pumpkins were making their annual appearance on porches and lawns along the highway. It reminded him that he'd need to schedule additional officers to handle the barrage of pranks that occurred around the thirty-first of the month. The kids in Sandwich seemed to get more creative every Halloween. Last year, a local man had found a pair of displaced geese from a nearby grist mill defiling the interior of his car which he had carelessly left unlocked. In spite of the man's efforts, his Chrysler had smelled like a migratory stop along the Atlantic flyway for months afterward.

Burroughs grinned widely as he crossed the tracks of the Cape Cod Scenic Railway and turned onto the road that would take him to his home on the marsh. Aside from the wind, it was a pretty quiet night.

But all that was about to change.

***

A few miles away a man and woman were arguing on an observation deck overlooking the entrance to the Cape Cod Canal. As the exchanges grew louder, their voices began to carry. Even in the stiff winds of the incoming frontal system, anyone standing in reasonable proximity could've heard them clearly. The woman pushed the man away from her.

"Keep your hands off me, Randall!"

"Oh, come on, Abby. You know you want to. The truth is we've never stopped loving each other. We were great together once and, if we try again, we can be even better."

"I don't want any of it. I don't want *you*."

The man moved toward her again and she backed away toward the steps that led to the boardwalk. "Believe me, if I had known what you had in mind, I would never have agreed to meet you here in the first place," she said.

"We can start over. Just give it a chance. You'll realize that deep down you still love me."

"Love you? Don't be ridiculous. Our marriage was a joke. I was never more than a piece of property to you."

The man raised his voice, his anger becoming apparent. "I gave you everything you have," he growled.

"The only thing you gave me was a Xanax dependency and a trip to the intensive care unit. I can see you're working yourself into one of your little rages right now. Love you? I *loathe* you, Randall. Go home and be with your things. I'm not one of them anymore."

The woman turned and quickly made her way down the steps to the parking lot below. The man shouted at her as she headed toward her car.

"Bitch."

He thought about following her but realized it was hopeless. He had blown any chance at reconciliation. She represented just one path to the desired objective. There was another option still in play.

Screw her, he thought.

Reaching into his jacket pocket he produced a cigarette, lit it and exhaled a billowy stream of smoke into the night.

Abigail Rhodes reached her car, a Subaru Outback, and fished the keys out of her purse. As she settled into the driver's seat, she cursed herself for agreeing to this little rendezvous. She glanced into the rear-view mirror, assessing what the winds of the cold front had done to her hair. It was then that she saw something move in the shadows behind her. Alarmed, she quickly locked all the doors and started the car. As she pulled onto the exit road, her headlights illuminated a tall figure approaching the boardwalk. The figure turned toward her, lifting a hand to shield its eyes from the halogen beams.

"A scarecrow?" she said out loud.

Abby's heart began to race. The figure looked like it had taken a detour off the Yellow Brick Road. Her anxiety abated somewhat when she realized that Halloween was only a week away. Perhaps the person in the costume had attended an early celebration.

She looked around for lights in nearby homes which would indicate that a late night party was still in progress. Odd, she thought. It was nearing midnight on a Wednesday. Not the usual time to host a costume party. There were no lights on in any of the houses. Most were just dark shapes against the angry sky.

She checked the rearview mirror again and caught a last glimpse of the outlandish figure making its way across the boardwalk before a turn in the road shifted her attention back to the lonely drive home. She chuckled to herself as she imagined the surprise her ex-husband had in store.

Back on the observation deck, Randall Landry was still agitated. He had been watching the rising surf on the bay since his ex-wife had stormed off. The wind had turned cooler and was pelting him with stinging sand. This served to exacerbate his foul mood. Things had not gone as planned. He had barely managed to restrain himself from throttling her again.

The bitch.

There were few women who could resist him. Who the hell did she think she was?

An ash from the cigarette blew into his face, burning his cheek.

"Shit," he cursed.

He crushed the cigarette out in the sand, vowing to return to a nicotine gum regimen. He really needed to quit smoking. As a plastic surgeon, he knew all too well that his pack-a-day habit would eventually cause unsightly wrinkles. A wrinkled practitioner of cosmetics would hardly inspire confidence in the rich, vain and aging female clients who sought eternal youth and he wasn't about to sacrifice a six figure salary.

Tonight, his careful planning had crashed and burned. He had been trying to get back into his ex-wife's good graces for months, but he had moved too fast and the proverbial door had slammed in his face. He wasn't interested in rekindling their marriage. Screw that. Now he needed money to get himself out of trouble—and quickly.

"This isn't over," he muttered aloud.

There was another lucrative source he could tap. He had already approached the individual. All he needed to do was apply the necessary pressure. Considering what was at stake, he was certain his monetary demands would be met. Though it would have been nice to lure his "ex" back into the sack, there were plenty of other women who would gladly satisfy his desires. To hell with that bitch and her bloated bankroll.

Randall reached into his jacket for the keys to his Mercedes. What he saw next was his last earthly image.

A smiley face crudely painted on burlap.

There was a series of wet, hacking sounds before his head dropped to the sand and rolled into the dune grass on its way to the beach below.

2

The *Dragnet* theme shattered the stillness of Burroughs' darkened bedroom. Having grown up with the show, it had seemed a fitting choice for a ringtone. Startled, Burroughs snapped on the light and fumbled with his old flip phone.

"Hello," he muttered.

"I was hoping you were home from Springfield, Chief."

The voice belonged to Annie Mullaney, a dispatcher for the Sandwich Police Department.

"Sorry to wake you, but we've got something you'll want to respond to."

"What time is it?"

"It's four twenty-five, Thom."

He yawned. "What've we got? I'm working on about three and a half hours of sleep here."

"There's a body out on the observation deck overlooking the Canal."

"That's practically in my backyard," he said, becoming abruptly alert.

Burroughs padded across the cold hardwood floor to his bedroom window. He could see the flashing lights of multiple squad cars across the marsh.

"That's why I called, Chief," Annie went on. "This is bad—really bad. One of your neighbors found the body while he was walking his dog. I didn't want to wake you at first so I sent Detective Barber with two other units to handle it. They're securing the scene."

"Do we know what happened to the victim?"

"He lost his head."

"Excuse me?"

"The body is headless. They haven't found it yet."

"Have you called the coroner?"

"She's en route."

"Who found the body?"

"Dave Stancyck."

"I don't know him."

"He lives a few hundred yards up the road from you. He works for an advertising firm in Boston. He was up early for the commute. Apparently, he's pretty shaken up."

"Did Fred have a chance to talk to him?"

"Yup. He didn't have any helpful details."

"Okay, Annie. Have them barricade the area from the bay beach entrance and throw up some crime scene tape on this side of the boardwalk. I'm on my way."

"Anything else, Chief?"

"Try to keep a lid on this as long as you can. I can do without the media cluster this'll turn into. As soon as I get a better idea of what happened out there, I'll brief Mayor Jerzowicz and toss the news stations a couple of bones."

"Okay, Chief."

"Thanks, Annie. Talk to you later."

Burroughs dressed, brushed his teeth, and debated whether to drive or walk to the crime scene. In the end, he decided that a brisk stroll in the cool October air would help wake him up. He unlocked his gun safe and strapped on his shoulder holster, a department-issued Glock. He threw on his Nautica sailing jacket, locked up the house, and headed down the long asphalt asphalt driveway to the private road that wound circuitously to the marsh.

Last night's wind had subsided, but the air was still brisk. Burroughs could see his breath. Near the boardwalk, one of his men was busy securing yellow crime scene tape across the walkway that led to the observation deck. The officer, a tall, gangly fellow who bore a striking resemblance to Ichabod Crane, looked up as Burroughs approached.

"Sorry, sir, but I'm afraid you can't enter the area right now."

"Officer Reynolds, it's Chief Burroughs."

Reynolds looked a bit embarrassed. "Oh sorry, Chief, I didn't recognize your face in the dark."

"No problem. When you finish with the tape, you can head back out on patrol. We've got three units here and we're going to need someone to handle morning traffic."

"You got it, Chief. Geez … a headless body. This is something we don't handle every day."

"Thank God for that, Ed."

Burroughs walked across the weathered planks and climbed the stairs to the overlook. He checked his watch, commending himself on making the trip from his house in only fifteen minutes. Detective Barber and a uniformed patrolman were standing beside the corpse. Burroughs noted that several sawhorses had been set up to block the parking lot entrance below. The sawhorses were flanked by a pair of patrol cars with their gumballs flashing insistently. It gave the scene a night club vibe.

Burroughs offered a cursory greeting and sent the patrolman—a short, paunchy guy named Viscoli—to the parking lot to impede any foot traffic from the boardwalk.

"We need to kill those lights," he told the officer. "We don't want to draw too much attention."

Viscoli nodded soberly. "Gotcha, Chief."

The scene was as gruesome as any Burroughs had ever laid eyes on and he had responded to a fair share of highway wrecks. The clothing indicated that the victim was likely a male, but with the head missing, it was just a reasonable guess. Burroughs pulled on a pair of latex gloves and asked the detective, "Fred, did you check for ID?"

"No. When Annie told me you were on the way, I figured you'd want the first look."

"That's fine. Let's have a peek. Annie wasn't kidding when she told me this was bad. Hey, you okay, Fred? I know this is pretty ugly."

"To tell you the truth, Chief, I think I might skip breakfast."

"No shame in that," Burroughs replied amicably, kneeling next to the victim. He moved the body gently, just enough to extract a wallet from the back pocket. He opened it and asked the detective for a flashlight. When the beam revealed the name and photo, Burroughs' eyes widened with surprise. He looked up at Barber then climbed to his feet.

"We've got a serious problem here. You need to call Annie. Tell her to contact the State Police and get their CSI unit here as quickly as possible."

"The coroner's already on the way, Chief."

"I know, Fred. Just do what I asked. Where's the guy who found the body?"

"His name's Stancyck. He's in Viscoli's car … with his dog."

"Okay. Did you get everything you needed from him?"

"Yeah. We've got his statement and contact info."

"Good. Let's see about sending him home then."

Burroughs led the way down the steps to the parking lot. Barber hurried to his own cruiser as the Chief headed off to Viscoli's unit. Following orders, Barber contacted Annie via the car radio and relayed the instructions he'd received.

"Why do we need the state CSI unit?" Annie said.

"The Chief got kinda spooked when he saw the vic's wallet."

"Really? Who is it?"

"Don't know. He didn't tell me."

"Did you see the name?"

"No. He slipped the wallet into his jacket like he was trying to hide it or something."

"Where is he now?"

"Talking with that Stancyck guy."

"This is getting really weird. All right. I'll get the state police there ASAP. Out."

Barber returned the speaker mic to its cradle and exited the vehicle. While Burroughs was busy with Stancyck, he figured he might poke around on the overlook for more clues as to the victim's identity.

After dismissing Stancyck, Burroughs walked to the Mercedes and tried the door on the passenger side. It was open. Using Barber's flashlight, he meticulously checked the interior of the car. The registration and insurance forms in the glove box indicated that the vehicle belonged to Randall Landry, MD, the same name on the license he had pulled from the victim's pocket. He returned the documents to the glove compartment and popped the trunk. Aside from a spare tire, jumper cables and a box of flares, there was nothing of interest.

Burroughs climbed back up the stairs to the overlook. Barber had produced a backup flashlight and was checking the area around the body.

"Fred, are you wearing gloves?"

"Of course, Chief."

"Could you check the victim for car keys?"

"Sure."

Barber patted the body down, quickly finding what he was looking for.

"They're in the right-hand pocket. Do you need them?"

"Nope. That's fine. Leave them where they are."

Keys on the victim's body indicated that he had driven himself to the beachside parking lot. But for what purpose? To meet someone? If so, who and why on such a gusty, chilly night? Burroughs knew Randall Landry all too well. They had a history and not a particularly good one.

Landry was among the leading surgeons on the East Coast—the favored cosmetic specialist among New England's rich and famous. He was widely known as a womanizer. Perhaps he had arranged to meet one of his latest conquests, a married woman with a jealous husband who had shown up instead. The savageness of the attack strongly suggested that this had been a crime of passion. Unless they were dealing with some deranged killer whose motives could not be clearly explained.

Headlights at the far end of the parking lot captured Burroughs' attention. He watched as the sawhorses were moved by the officer on guard and a Subaru Outback was waved through. He recognized the car immediately and hurried down the steps to greet the Sandwich Coroner.

"Hello, Thom," she said.

"Hello, Doctor Rhodes," he replied. "I'm afraid I have some bad news for you."

3

Doctor Abigail Rhodes had pulled her hair into a ponytail and was dressed in casual street clothes, indicating her haste in traveling to the Sandwich marsh from her home in Bourne at such an hour. She looked at the Mercedes then back at Burroughs before she said gravely, "The body on the overlook is Randall's, isn't it?"

Burroughs watched tears form in the Doctor's eyes. He nodded.

"I was here with him a few hours ago," she admitted, struggling to keep her composure. "We had an awful fight. God, Thom ... I can't believe this."

"I've got a state police team on the way," he told her sympathetically. "You don't have to go up there."

"I need to do my job," she said.

"Doctor, considering your divorce and the media circus that followed, I don't think it's a good idea. The press would have a field day. It's going to be bad enough as it is."

"I'm not a suspect am I?"

"Of course not. But I need to know why you were here. There's still a restraining order in place, isn't there?"

"No," she told him. "We came to an agreement because of something that happened at the clinic."

Abby had opened a community health care center with some of the dividends her divorce settlement had provided. The clinic catered to underprivileged local residents—seasonal workers without benefits mostly. Living on Cape Cod was expensive and these people were barely making ends meet. Thanks to Abby's tireless efforts, physicians from all over Massachusetts were pooling their time and resources to provide affordable health care to the Cape's working poor. Annual fundraising campaigns helped keep the clinic running.

"Thom, do you remember the kid who was so badly disfigured in that accident on Route 28 this past summer?"

"I do."

"We had run out of options for his continued treatment when Randall called me out of the blue and offered his services gratis."

Burroughs was genuinely surprised. "Are you sure we're talking about the same Randall Landry you were married to?"

"I was pretty shocked myself. He wanted absolutely no publicity. He performed two procedures at his private suite in Boston. Apparently, his father assisted both times. When the boy's bandages came off, the results were miraculous. During the treatment, Randall and I discussed the case several times and found ourselves on surprisingly friendly terms. In order to work together, I had to waive the restraining order."

"I see," said Burroughs. "So how long have you been in contact with him?"

"He called me a few months ago … said he'd changed since the divorce and hoped we could be friends. After the second operation, he volunteered to take on more cases at the clinic."

"Well, that's highly out of character," Burroughs remarked.

"I know," she agreed. "But he sounded so sincere. He asked me to dinner to discuss the arrangement and, well, I jumped at the opportunity. Not because I wanted to rekindle anything of course. But the clinic is always in need of talented surgeons."

"I understand. So you went out with him last night?"

"Yes."

"How'd it go?"

"Like I said, it was a train wreck. We met at Chillingworth's in Brewster. I had a little wine with dinner. He asked if I wanted to drive out to the overlook. I agreed on the condition that I take my own car. I don't know what I was thinking, really. I loved him once. And I do admire his surgical skills. But I should have known he had ulterior motives."

"When did you leave the restaurant?"

"Sometime after eleven. We were the last table in the place. Randall has always been so entitled, he ignored all the hints from the wait staff that it was time to pay the bill."

"Was he drunk?"

"No. I don't think so."

"So you both drove out here?"

"Yeah. It was a little scary. There was no one around. The wind had come up and it was pretty cold out. Randall started hitting on me and getting free with his hands."

Her voice trailed off.

"Did he hurt you?" Burroughs inquired.

"No. But he gave me a pretty good scare. I could tell he was getting worked up. He was always so volatile. I dealt with that for years."

"I understand. Any idea what time you left?"

"No. I was pretty upset. I just wanted to get home."

"Did you notice anyone else around as you were leaving?"

"Yes. I was going to tell you about that. After I got into my car, I saw a person dressed as a scarecrow walking through the parking lot."

Burroughs raised an eyebrow. "A scarecrow—really?"

"I know. I thought it was weird, too. Halloween isn't until next week and every house I saw on the marsh was dark except for a few outdoor lights."

"This isn't really a late night community," Burroughs explained. "We're all in bed by ten o'clock most nights. The nearest bar is out on Route 6A."

"You live here?" She inquired.

"Yeah, about a mile or so up the road."

"Nice," she commented.

There was a short break in the conversation. The sun would not be making an appearance for quite a while, but the air was beginning to warm up considerably. In the distance, waves crashed on the shore of the bay. There was no sign of the state police yet. Burroughs pondered the conundrum of the scarecrow, searching for logical explanations. Abby's attention shifted to the observation deck.

"Doctor Rhodes—" He began.

"Thom, when it's just you and me, call me Abby for God's sake. I appreciate the courtesy, but we've been working together for years."

"Right. Didn't mean to be so formal," he said apologetically. "About that scarecrow of yours, I'm thinking maybe there was a party at one of those bars on 6A. I can check around. Someone could have left the bar all liquored up and decided to walk home to avoid a DUI."

"It's an awfully long walk from 6A around the marsh."

"Might not seem like it to a drunk person."

"That's true," she agreed, glancing apprehensively up the stairs. "I'm wrestling with some serious guilt, here, Thom. My ex-husband is lying dead up on the overlook and somehow I don't really feel all that bad about it."

"It's completely understandable," he said in a reassuring tone.

"Before the state police get here, can I take a quick look at the scene?"

"It's not a good idea, Abby. You can't be involved in this investigation."

"I don't plan on investigating," she told him. "I just need to see him."

"All right," he agreed.

They mounted the stairs to the overlook. A thin line of crimson and purple indicated that a new day was about to begin on Cape Cod. Barber was leaning over the railing staring into the bay. There were coin operated binoculars on either side of the observation deck. Landry's body lay sprawled between opposing wooden benches. Barber offered a greeting as Abby and the Chief made an appearance.

"Morning, Doctor Rhodes."

"Morning, Detective."

Burroughs saw no sense in being coy about the victim's identity any longer. "Fred, the Doctor won't be participating in this investigation. The victim is her ex-husband."

Barber was caught off guard. "Oh. I'm … sorry," he said. "Do you need some privacy?"

Abby shook her head. "No. But thank you, Detective."

She didn't look like the stoic professional Burroughs had evaluated so many horrific scenes with. She looked vulnerable and shaken. Even under these unfortunate circumstances, Burroughs couldn't help admiring her beauty. She was a petite woman in her mid-forties who had cheated time without the ministrations of her ex-husband's surgical skills. She could easily have passed for a woman ten years younger.

In striking contrast, the body on the deck was ghastly to look at. The head had been severed and the stump looked curiously like a flank steak. Blood had pooled beneath it and congealed on the wooden planks. Even with all her professional experience, it was quite a shock to Abby, who instinctively put a hand over her mouth.

"My God … who could have done this?" she gasped.

"Are you all right, Doctor?" Burroughs asked compassionately. "You look a little pale."

Before she could answer, a procession of state police vehicles arrived at the parking lot entrance.

"We've got to get off this dune, Abby. The cavalry's here."

4

The sun was still below the horizon as Abby and Thom watched a lab truck accompanied by two state cruisers converge upon the scene. After gaining access through the barricades, the vehicles rumbled to a stop in front of the lookout stairs. Inside one of the squad cars, a uniformed trooper was engaged in an animated discussion on his mobile radio unit. Beside him, a heavy-set man in a gray trench coat was polishing off the remains of a glazed donut. A donut, thought Burroughs derisively.

The trench coat man exited the cruiser and immediately began barking out orders to his associates. A pair of forensic officers hurried up the steps past Abby and Thom. The Trench Coat Man addressed Burroughs without introducing himself.

"That the vic's vehicle?" he asked, glancing at the Mercedes in the lot.

"Yes," said Burroughs, offering his hand. "I'm—"

Trench Coat Man looked right through him. "You been over it?"

"Yes."

"Get an ID?"

Burroughs pulled Landry's wallet from his jacket pocket and handed it over. "This was on the victim," he explained. "Papers in the glove compartment indicate that the car belongs to him."

Trench Coat Man regarded the wallet dully. After a few seconds, he looked up at Abby. "Who's she?"

"Doctor Abigail Rhodes. She's our coroner. She also happens to be the victim's ex-wife."

"I see," said Trench Coat Man.

"I'm fully capable of speech," Abby quipped.

"Okay. Did you get a look at the body, Miss Rhodes?"

"You can call me Doctor," she corrected him.

"Right. Did you get a look at the vic, Doc?"

"I've removed her from this investigation," Burroughs interjected. "Conflict of interest. That's why I called you guys."

"Oh," Trench Coat Man said. "So aside from that, you figured you guys could handle this locally."

Burroughs gritted his teeth. "Maybe it's time you told us who you are," he said irritably.

"Lieutenant David Carlson, District Four CSI."

"You're stationed out of Bourne, right?"

"That's right."

Those words had no sooner been spoken when a startled shout emanated from the area beneath the lookout.

"Oh, shit! I almost tripped right over the goddamn thing."

Burroughs fixed Carlson with a smug look. "You might want to go check that out. It appears as if one of your men just found the victim's head."

5

After another round of questioning, Carlson excused himself to survey the carnage on the observation deck. "I'll need to speak with both of you in more detail when we're finished combing the area," he informed them.

"Lieutenant, if you're going to be a while, do you have any objection to us grabbing a little breakfast?" Burroughs asked.

"I could use a cup of coffee and a donut, myself. Here, let me give you some money."

Unbelievable, Burroughs thought. "No worries," he offered. "I got it. Here, let me give you my cell phone number in case you need answers while we're gone."

Carlson tapped the number into his Android phone. "Appreciate it," he said, making his way toward the stairs.

When he was gone, Abby muttered, "More donuts—seriously?"

Burroughs chuckled. "Are you up for breakfast? I hope I wasn't being presumptuous."

"I could always eat," she said. "It's a wonder I'm not three hundred and fifty pounds."

"We'll have to take your car. Mine's back at the house."

"That's fine."

As they strolled across the parking lot, the conversation inevitably turned toward the matter at hand.

"So who do you think would want to kill Randall?" Burroughs wondered.

"I don't know. But I was an idiot to think he cared about that kid from the clinic. I can't believe I allowed myself to get sucked back in."

"Don't beat yourself up. Do you think he had motives beyond rekindling your relationship?"

"It certainly wouldn't surprise me."

"What do you think they could have been?"

"I'm not sure," she said, removing the key fob from the pocket of her navy blue hoodie, "but I know that Randall would never do anything unless there was something in it for him."

She pointed the fob at the Subaru and it made a loud chirping noise. The headlights flickered once. She continued talking as the two of them climbed into her car.

"He wasn't even all that invested in his patients. He went through the motions, of course. And he could really turn on the charm when he was attracted to a particular female client. But for the most part, he was only in it for the money. That and continued exposure in the *American Journal of Cosmetic Surgery*."

Abby started the car and pulled out of the parking lot past the sawhorse barricade. Burroughs' local sentry had been replaced by a state trooper who looked tired and a little bored. Overhead, a noisy flock of seagulls wheeled about, changed course and headed toward the fishing boats making their way to the piers along the Canal.

"So where are we going?" Abby wondered.

"I don't know. Do you have any place in mind?"

"The Marshland is pretty good," she said.

"Works for me," he told her.

The Marshland was usually packed even in the off season. The breakfast specials were simple yet creative and the homemade muffins were considered by many to be the best on the Cape. Getting in and out quickly wasn't always possible, but Burroughs was pretty sure the state police would be tied up for quite a while. Besides, Carlson had his number if anything pressing came up.

Though Burroughs had been working alongside Abby for a long time, he couldn't remember participating in anything overtly social with her. Any breakfast they had previously shared had been hastily grabbed from a drive-thru window. He felt a little nervous suddenly. He had sequestered himself from the dating scene after the tragic death of his wife and daughter which had led to his relocation from Monterey, California. Over the past ten years, he had completely immersed himself in work. The prospect of dating was completely alien to him. This wasn't a date anyway. It was an investigation.

So why was he feeling so awkward?

He was out of practice, he supposed. He hadn't been to a restaurant with a woman in eons and this one was particularly attractive. All right, get it together here, Chief, he told himself. This isn't the prom.

Abby noted the odd expression on Burroughs' face. Though he had always been very personable with her, he tended to be a bit inaccessible. He seemed haunted somehow and she wondered if some terrible event had made him that way. There was a tenderness about him. She had seen him offer comforting words to frightened children and grieving spouses. But she had also witnessed his wrath, especially on the night Randall had beaten her within inches of her life. Burroughs had been the responding officer on the scene. When Randall had told Burroughs to "mind his own fucking business" and thrown an ill-advised punch, Burroughs had dropped him with a single blow. Later, he had brought her flowers in the intensive care unit. The fact that he was both tough and sensitive enhanced her overall opinion of him. She found him extremely easy to be around.

Along Shore Road, a kid on a bicycle was delivering the *Cape Cod Times*. He darted out in front of the Subaru, prompting Abby to hastily apply the brakes. The kid patted his chest as if to say *my bad* then continued on his way.

"I didn't know that kids even delivered papers anymore," Abby said.

"Out on the marsh, there's an old guy who brings them in a beat-up Cadillac. The houses are so far apart, you know?"

"Yeah, that makes sense," she replied. "Most people get their news on the internet these days."

"That's unfortunate if you ask me," he remarked. "Too many people mistake opinions for fact. Thanks to the social media, folks have come to rely less on dependable news sources and more on the rantings of random bloggers. We're a nation of catch phrases and sound bites taken out of context. And what's worse, no one seems to care."

"Sounds like you've given this a lot of thought," she said.

"There are a few things that make my blood boil and that's one of them. Kids and their smartphones … now that's a whole other issue. Don't even get me going on that."

She chuckled. "You're a man of passion, Thom."

"Nah. Mostly I'm just an old fart," he joked.

They both laughed at that one and then rode in comfortable silence the rest of the way.

***

Abby parked the car in the nearest available space and they exited the vehicle. Though it was shortly before 6 a.m., the restaurant was busy already with morning commuters heading toward Boston. They were greeted warmly by a bustling waitress and told that they could seat themselves at any available table. They chose a window seat facing a small park across the street.

When they had settled in Abby remarked, "I know exactly what I'm getting already."

"Do you come here for breakfast a lot?" He wondered.

"Often enough. The cranberry muffins are to die for."

"I would have figured you for a more upscale kind of gal," he confessed.

"Why, because my ex-husband took me to Chillingworth's last night? Don't get me wrong, that place is wonderful, but I've always been more comfortable with the casual dining thing."

"Good to know," he said. "Speaking of your ex, what was your impression of the murder scene?"

"The wind last night played hell with the area around the dune, but from the angle of the cuts and the position of the body, it's likely that Randall was standing when he was attacked. The ragged nature of the wound suggests that it took several blows to remove the head. The killer must have used something large and extremely sharp."

"Like a machete?"

"Yeah, or maybe a sickle."

"A sickle?"

"You know, one of those things that were used to harvest crops back in the day."

"Like the grim reaper uses," he added.

"Actually, the reaper uses a scythe," she corrected him. "It's got a much longer handle."

"You're right," he replied. "Scarecrows are sometimes pictured with sickles. Was the guy in the costume holding one?"

She shuddered, feeling a sudden chill. "Not that I noticed."

The waitress arrived and offered them menus. Burroughs told her they were both ready to order—a cranberry muffin and black coffee for Abby, corned beef hash with two sunny-side up eggs for Thom. She thanked them and hustled off to the kitchen with the ticket.

"You know, I never thanked you for visiting me in the hospital," she said, changing the subject.

"You didn't need to," he told her. "It was something I wanted to do."

"But you didn't have to and I appreciate it."

"Okay," he said, shifting uncomfortably in his seat. "You're welcome, then."

"I still think about that night sometimes. Randall had gotten angry before, but I'd never seen him so worked up. I wonder what would have happened if you hadn't come rushing into the house. He might have killed me I suppose."

Her voice trailed off weakly. She cleared her throat.

"And then there was the divorce," she went on. "Our hearing got almost as much coverage as the Bruins and Patriots. I seem to remember you helped keep the media hounds at bay a time or two. I never thanked you for that, either."

He waved a hand at her dismissively. "It was nothing. You were being harassed and I was just doing my job."

"Do you ever take credit for anything, Thom?"

"Not usually," he admitted, obviously ill at ease with this sort of attention.

The waitress dropped off coffee for Abby and a glass of water for Thom. He stuck his straw in and began sipping it thirstily.

"Anyway, you're pretty handy to have around. I'll think I'll keep you," she concluded.

"Thanks," he said.

His cell phone went off then.

"You have the Dragnet theme as a ring tone?" She asked, mildly amused.

He smiled at her. "Yup. I better take this."

It was Carlson, officious as ever. "You and the Doc need to get back here. Our sweep of the area didn't turn up much, other than the head that is." He shouted at somebody. "Hey, get that goddamn thing outta here. Yeah, you—genius! Christ, it's hard to find good help nowadays."

"Problems?" Burroughs inquired glibly.

"You don't know the half of it. Hey, listen, Burroughs, don't forget about the coffee and the donut okay? I like my coffee black. I'm not too picky about my donuts."

"Okay," Burroughs replied. But the lieutenant had already hung up. "We need to get back to the scene," he told Abby.

"So our little date is over?"

"Is that what this was?" He joked.

"Of course not," she teased. "If this were a date I would have worn something unforgettable."

"What you have on is working just fine," he said, worrying slightly that he had overstepped his boundaries.

Her warm smile told him he hadn't.

6

Back at the overlook, forensic officers were loading Randall's remains into a lab truck. The body had been placed inside a black plastic bag. One of the officers was holding a smaller container that resembled a bowling bag. Abby shuddered when she realized what was in it. As the door of the lab truck slammed shut, a number of seagulls combing the area for scraps were startled into flight. Carlson, who had been standing behind the door, suddenly appeared in full view. Burroughs offered the lieutenant a Styrofoam cup which contained coffee he presumed was lukewarm at best by now. He smiled sarcastically and said, "Would you believe they were out of donuts?"

"No problem," Carlson replied, prying open the lid and taking a swig. Some of it dribbled down his chin and he wiped his face with the back of his hand. "Were they out of napkins, too?"

Burroughs shrugged as Carlson turned his attention to Abby.

"Doctor Rhodes, you mentioned earlier that you met your husband here last night."

"Ex-husband," she corrected him.

"Right, your ex. I need you to go over the details of that meeting."

Carlson's second sip of coffee produced the same results. Annoyed, he handed it to a passing lab tech who eyed it suspiciously before walking off with it.

Abby repeated her entire story, including details about the clinic and the operations Randall had performed on the disfigured boy in Boston. When she got to the part about the man in the scarecrow costume, Carlson appeared skeptical.

"A scarecrow … are you sure?"

"Yeah, it was kinda hard to miss. My headlights were shining right on him."

"You keep saying *him*," Carlson pointed out. "How do you know it was a man?"

"He was extremely tall and I could tell by the way he walked."

"All right. So where was this scarecrow headed?"

"I don't know," she answered. "He was heading toward the boardwalk in the direction of the lookout."

"So you never saw him climb the stairs?"

"No. And at that moment, I just wanted to get out of there quick. I was upset and a little startled."

"Yeah, I can see how you would be," Carlson validated her. "Guy in a scarecrow costume wandering around in the dark … that's pretty weird." He shifted his gaze to Burroughs. "Are there any bars in proximity?"

"Nearest one's on Route 6A," Burroughs answered. "It's a long walk from here. A couple of miles if you follow the side road. Much shorter if you cut through the marsh."

"Why would anybody do that?"

"Good question," Burroughs said. "Especially during high tide."

"One of our guys found some motorcycle tracks in the sand on the marsh side of the parking lot," Carlson announced, turning his attention back to Abby. "You don't recall seeing a motorcycle around last night, do you?"

"No," Abby answered quickly. But then something did occur to her. "Wait … when Randall and I left the restaurant there was a motorcycle behind us on 6A. I guess I didn't think anything of it at the time."

"Hmm," said Carlson, processing the information. "How long was the bike following you?"

"I never said it was following us, though I guess it could have been."

"I don't suppose the rider was wearing a scarecrow costume."

"All I saw was a single headlight and a silhouette."

Burroughs joined the conversation then. "Lieutenant, I was planning on checking out the local bars to see if any of them were throwing a costume party last night."

"That's a good idea. Let me know what you find out."

"I will."

Carlson fumbled around in his coat for business cards. When he had located them, he handed one to Burroughs and another to Abby. "How tall are you, Doctor Rhodes?" He asked her.

"Five-foot-one," she told him.

"Looks like you're off the hook for your ex-husband's murder. My techs all agree that, based on the angle of the wound, the assailant had to have been well over six-feet tall and unusually strong. It takes a lot of power to lop off a guy's head."

"Was my innocence ever in doubt?" Abby wondered.

Carlson didn't answer.

"So, what are they thinking the killer used as a weapon?" Burroughs inquired.

"It had to have been something fairly sharp. Whatever it was, it had a curved blade."

"Like a sickle you mean?" Abby proposed.

Carlson considered the possibility. "Yeah, I suppose that would have worked. Did your scarecrow have one on him?"

"Not that I saw."

"The scarecrow could be irrelevant to the case," Carlson commented. "Or maybe he's our guy. You know of any costume shops around here?"

"There's one in Orleans," Burroughs told him.

"And another in Plymouth," added Abby.

"Those are good places to start. I'll have my guys look into it," Carlson said to Burroughs. "In the meantime, you can check out the local watering holes and see if any of them were hosting a Halloween party last night."

"Sounds good," Burroughs agreed.

"Anything I can do?" Abby offered.

"It'd be a good idea if you stayed out of the way," Carlson advised her. "Landry kept a pretty high profile. Just about everyone in New England has heard a little something about your divorce. That was quite a charitable gesture on your part, opening that clinic. Affordable healthcare is hard to come by nowadays."

"It is," she said, somewhat flattered by the remark.

"Well, I think we're about done here, Chief. Do you want to notify the next of kin or should I?"

"Might be better if you handled it," Burroughs explained. "The Landrys and I have a bit of a history."

"Oh?"

"When Randall put Abby in the hospital a few years ago, I was the responding officer. It got a little rough and I had to lay him out. He threatened to sue the department. Hired his father's lawyer — some hotshot from Cambridge. It was a bit of a mess."

"I see. I'll have my guys take care of it then. How are you going to handle the media when this story breaks, Chief?"

"I'm going to get in touch with the Mayor and let him decide."

"Yeah, It's usually best to defer to the top," Carlson agreed. "I'll keep you apprised of any new developments. I expect you'll do the same." Turning toward Abby, he added, "Doctor Rhodes, I'm sorry for your loss." Then he abruptly sauntered away.

7

On the ride back to Thom's house, Abby was brooding a little. She wasn't accustomed to being excluded from an investigation and was feeling rather useless.

"What's wrong?" Thom asked, sensing her sour mood.

"I'm not good at being a spectator."

"I know," he sympathized. "But I imagine the autopsy would have been pretty difficult for you."

"I didn't take this job because it was easy," she remarked.

They were quiet for a while after that.

The road on either side of them was thick with marsh reeds and bulrushes. "There's a mailbox coming up on your right," Thom informed her. "You're going to want to slow down or you'll fly right past my driveway. It's a real challenge turning around on this road."

She could see how that would be true. The road was little more than a single lane and there was no shoulder. Stray too far off the path and you'd end up in the marsh. She slowed to a crawl until she spotted a paved opening in the foliage.

"This is it," he announced.

She pulled to a stop and stared gloomily into the distance. "Thom, I hope this isn't too forward of me, but would you mind if I came in for a minute? I know you've got a million things to do, but ...," she swallowed hard, feeling a sudden wave of emotion, "I just don't feel like being alone right now."

"Of course," he said. He could see that she was fighting back tears. He could only imagine the internal conflict she must be wrestling with. Such a brutal murder. Nobody deserved to die that way, even a philandering, pompous bully like Randall. "Do you drink tea?" He asked her.

"I do," she told him.

"Okay. I'll make you some. Just follow the driveway up to the house."

Thom's home lay at the crest of a gentle slope. It was a modest saltbox cottage with cedar shakes that were well-weathered by the ocean wind. Enormous windows in front provided a panoramic view of the marsh and ocean beyond. A raised-bed garden in the side lot was surrounded by a white picket fence. The garden was well stocked with autumn flowers still in bloom—dahlias, salvias, and mums. Abby thought of the twenty-room monstrosity she had shared with her ex-husband. Even with five thousand-plus square feet, it lacked the character and charm of Thom's tidy home.

"This is beautiful," she remarked.

"Thanks," he said humbly. "It was a little run down when I bought it. I did most of the upgrades myself. I added about seven-hundred square feet."

"So, you're pretty handy, huh?"

"I learned a little from my dad. He was a carpenter by trade. I worked for him to pay my way through college."

"Nice. Is your father still alive?"

"No," Thom answered a bit wistfully. "Both of my parents passed a few years ago."

"I'm sorry," Abby offered. "That's hard on any kid at any age."

"It is," he agreed. "I still miss them sometimes. What about you — are your parents still around?"

"They are, but they don't live on the Cape. They moved to Florida a while back."

"Sun worshippers, eh?"

"Yup. Works for some people I suppose. But I've always loved the changing of the seasons."

"Me, too," he said. "We get our fair share of rough winters here, but I wouldn't trade it for anything."

There was a carport on the side of the house. It was wide enough to accommodate two vehicles. Thom's Jeep was parked closest to the entryway, which had a barn-style door with wrought iron hinges. He told Abby to pull her Subaru into the open space. She did as instructed, thinking about how nice it would be to own a place like this. Currently, she occupied a two bedroom townhouse in one of those cookie-cutter housing developments in Bourne. It was fairly upscale but completely devoid of personality.

A neatly trimmed row of privet hedges separated the carport from the backyard. Abby could see that the yard was filled with a series of flower beds and rock gardens, all connected by winding flagstone paths. It was evident that Thom spent a lot of time outdoors. One of the paths led to a charming little building with cedar shakes and white shutters. She assumed it was a guest house.

"Should have grabbed the newspaper when we were down at the end of the driveway," Thom muttered as he keyed in through the side door.

Abby followed him through a mud room into a country style kitchen with a breakfast bar. She marveled at the amount of counter space — something her own kitchen was sorely lacking. An oval pot rack above the island was well stocked with all sorts of exotic looking pans and utensils.

"Do you cook?" She asked him.

"I dabble a little," he told her. "Good food is one of my passions."

"Me, too," she professed.

He reached into a drawer and pulled out a wooden tea box stocked with a wide variety of exotic blends. "Have a seat," he invited her. "I'll put the kettle on. I hope you find something you like in there."

It didn't take her long. She chose a green tea with a citrus blend and seated herself on a stool at the breakfast bar. After Thom had started the stove, he grabbed a matching pair of coffee mugs from a handsome glass cabinet and placed them in front of Abby. "I think I'll join you," he said, sifting through the box of tea. He complimented her on her choice and selected a package of the same blend. "That is a good one," he assured her.

She smiled at him as he sat at the stool across from her.

"What?" Thom said, taken off guard.

"Nothing," she answered. "It's just that this is really ... nice."

"Thanks. I don't have company very often."

"You should," she said. "It's a shame to keep a house like this all to yourself."

He nodded and smiled politely

"Thanks for having me in," she went on. "I feel so strange about all this."

"I can imagine."

"It's not like I still have feelings for Randall. In fact, I found him extremely difficult to be around. Like I told you before, I only tolerated him because I knew he was a valuable asset to the clinic. But in spite of his abrasive personality traits, I just can't imagine who'd want to kill him in such a horrible way."

The kettle started whistling and Thom fetched it from the stove. He filled both mugs and placed a tea bag in each. Abby continued venting.

"You were right when you said the autopsy would have been hard for me. I realize I don't owe Randall anything, but still, I feel obligated to find out who killed him. Does that make sense?"

"Believe me, it does," he assured her.

The Dragnet theme interrupted their conversation. Thom pulled the offending cell phone from his pocket and checked the number. "It's Annie," he said apologetically, "I have to take this."

Annie's nasally voice made her sound like the archetypal small town telephone operator. "Where are you, Chief?"

"At home. I had to stop here to pick up my vehicle. What's up?"

"Officer Reynolds just checked in. Somebody drove off without paying at the Citgo station on 6A."

"Okay," Burroughs said flatly. "That's kind of a no-brainer. Have them check their security cams for a license plate so Reynolds can run the numbers."

"Yeah, they're already working on it, Chief. That's not why I'm calling."

There was a pause. She could be maddeningly slow about getting to the point sometimes.

"What's going on, Annie?" He prompted her.

"The attendant had the radio tuned to WXTK. During a news break, they mentioned that a body was found out on the marsh in Sandwich."

"Doesn't take them long, does it? Did they give any details?"

"Nope. But I'm sure the mayor is out of bed by now. He's going to want to know about this before he gets caught with his pants down."

"You're right, Annie. Thanks for the heads up. Would you happen to have his home number?"

He could hear papers being shuffled around.

"Yup, here it is. Ready? It's 775-6061."

There was a small pile of mail on the breakfast bar. Burroughs jotted the number down on one of the envelopes. "Thanks. I'll definitely give him a buzz. Let me know if there are any other developments. I've got a few things I need to follow up on before I head to the station. I'll be in as soon as I can."

"Okay, Chief. Sounds good. I'll keep you posted."

"Bye, Annie."

He snapped the phone shut and let out a heavy sigh. "And so it begins," he muttered.

Abby felt suddenly guilty. She had been so wrapped up in her own troubles, she hadn't realized that this might be an imposition to Thom.

The man had a lot on his plate at the moment. "I'm sure you've got a long day ahead of you," she said ruefully, "and I'm in your way. I should probably go."

"No," Burroughs insisted. "You're fine. Stay and drink your tea."

"Thanks," she countered, "but I know when it's my cue to leave. I probably shouldn't have invited myself in, to begin with."

Thom placed his hand on her arm and fixed her with a reassuring gaze. "Abby, you're shaken up and it's totally understandable. I'm happy to be the guy you vent to. It's okay … really."

She found some comfort in those words. "All right," she said. "One cup of tea and I'll be out of your hair."

"No rush," he assured her. "I do need to make a call, though. Would you excuse me?"

She nodded as he retreated to a private corner of the house. When he was gone, she enjoyed a few sips of tea while admiring her surroundings. A photo on the refrigerator captured her attention. It was fastened with a magnet bearing the seal of the Sandwich police department. In the photo, Thom was standing alongside a woman possibly in her mid-thirties and a girl of elementary school age. Both were brunettes with stunning blue eyes. The three of them looked very happy together. She wondered if Thom had a family somewhere. If so, he had never mentioned them. And he wore no wedding ring, either. Divorced, maybe? She felt a little nosy contemplating the possibilities. Whoever those people were, they were absolutely none of her business.

Abby was a bit startled when Thom suddenly appeared in the kitchen. He realized immediately what was occupying her attention.

"My wife and daughter," he offered.

"Oh," she said, trying to sound casual about it. "They're both very pretty."

"Yes, they were," he replied in a guarded tone.

She couldn't stop herself from prying a little. "Did something happen to them?"

"They were killed about twelve years ago … a hit and run."

Awkward, she thought, should have left well enough alone.

"Thom, that-that's awful," she said. "I'm sorry. I didn't mean to—"

"It's okay," he told her. "That picture was taken in Monterey where we used to live. The case was never solved so I've never had any real closure. My supervisor at the precinct wouldn't let me investigate it."

He clearly wasn't comfortable with the subject so she let it drop. There was an awkward silence as she sipped her tea.

"I just got off the phone with the Mayor," Thom said finally, "He wants me and Carlson to host a press conference."

"That Carlson's a real charmer," Abby remarked sarcastically. "He ought to be good for a few printable quotes."

"A journalist's dream," Thom agreed, chuckling.

She finished what was left of her tea in a couple of gulps and stood up to leave.

"Well, Chief, you've got a lot on your itinerary and I don't want to hold you up any longer. Thanks for letting me inside your home. It's lovely."

Clearing his throat, he said softly, "Maybe when this is all over, you can stop by again."

"I'd like that," she told him, heading toward the door.

He followed her through the mudroom into the carport. After exchanging goodbyes, he stood and watched her descend the driveway. As she disappeared from view, he thought, I should have had her over a long time ago.

8

Burroughs placed the coffee mugs in the sink to be cleaned later and checked his watch. It was 7:55. Most of the local drinking establishments wouldn't be open until eleven. He needed answers before then. Hoping to save himself the footwork, he decided to place a call to his good friend, Paul McCleod.

A giant of a man at six-foot-six, two-hundred-seventy pounds, Paul owned the Laughing Gull Pub in Dennis. On first glance, most people were intimidated by him. But he had a playful sense of humor and treated his customers like family. Paul's grandparents had immigrated to the States from Ireland during the 1920s. They opened the pub in 1947 and it had remained in the family ever since. In addition to the standard Irish fare such as fish and chips, shepherd's pie and beef stew, the place was known for its delicious grilled sandwiches. Burroughs' favorite was the Molly Malloy, which combined turkey, coleslaw and Swiss cheese with creamy Thousand Island dressing. It came with a generous portion of sweet potato fries. Thom usually washed it down with Paul's own microbrew, which was appropriately named McLeod's Ale. Traditional Irish singers and dancers kept patrons entertained during the summer months. In the offseason, it was the food and wide variety of authentic Irish brews that kept the locals coming back.

Paul had grown up in the pub. His parents used to joke that he had been conceived in it as well. He had started out delivering food and bussing tables at the age of twelve. During his mid-teens, he had worked his way up to the position of short order cook. After high school, he turned down a football scholarship at Boston University to take over the family business. Having made a small fortune over the years, he had no regrets.

Burroughs began frequenting Paul's establishment shortly after relocating to the Cape. With their mutual love of food, sports and beer, the two had become fast friends. Paul owned a small fishing boat and he took Thom out on it frequently. Their catches became daily specials at the pub on a regular basis.

No one was more familiar with the bar scene on Cape Cod than Paul. Though he definitely occupied his own little niche, he made a point of knowing what his peers were up to. It was smart business. If any of his competitors had been throwing a costume party within fifty miles of his place last night, Paul would know about it.

Burroughs found Paul's home number among his list of cell phone contacts and dialed it. It rang several times before Paul answered, sounding as if he had just rolled out of bed.

"This better be good."

"Sorry, am I interrupting prayer hour at your New England Patriots shrine?"

Paul's interest in football bordered on the obsessive and Burroughs never tired of razzing him about it.

"Hey, we missed you at the pub last night," Paul chuckled. "I thought you were going to stop by."

The *we* included Paul's wife Karee and daughter, Molly. They both worked at the restaurant and were dear friends of Thom's.

"I really wanted to," Thom explained, "but the seminar I was at ran late and there was a massive backup on the Pike. I didn't even hit the Cape until around eleven."

"Too bad for you," Paul said. "You missed out on a tasty batch of lobster bisque."

"Karee's recipe?"

"Of course."

"Ouch. You really know how to hurt a guy," Thom said.

"So why don't you give up your silly crime-fighting gig and take a job at Wal-Mart?"

"If I worked at Wal-Mart, I wouldn't be able to afford Karee's lobster bisque."

"That's true," Paul conceded, chuckling heartily.

"Hey, I've got a quick question for you," said Thom, getting down to business. "Do you know of any local bars that were hosting costume parties last night?"

There was a short pause as Paul considered the question.

"Hmm. No. That's not much of a draw on a Wednesday night with Halloween still a week away."

"That's kinda what I figured. Are you sure?"

"Yeah. If it was happening anywhere on this end of the Cape, I'd have heard about it. But you never know what's going on up in P-Town. Half of the population is in drag every day so ...."

"P-Town" was local slang for Provincetown—a notoriously free-spirited community at the northernmost tip of the Cape. Local residents exhibited a wide variety of sexual orientations and gender preferences. But the town was located nearly sixty miles from Sandwich, an impossible trek on foot and well over an hour by car. Burroughs found it highly unlikely that someone would travel such a considerable distance from a costume gala to commit a grisly murder at a secluded location on the Lower Cape.

"Okay, thanks, Paul. I appreciate it. I'm sorry if I woke you up."

"Don't worry about it. I'm here for you anytime. Let me know when you have a free Sunday. We'll see if those winter flounder are running again. And don't be a stranger to the pub. I'll have the kitchen staff set you up with something nice. Why did you want to know—"

"Thanks, Paul. I'm looking forward to it. Take care."

"You, too. Bye."

9

Abby was facing an unfamiliar dilemma—what to do with her day. Since her services were not required at the moment, she figured it was as good a time as any to stop by the clinic and see how things were going. She had removed herself from its daily operations years ago but still served as a managing consultant when her schedule allowed. Located in Hyannis, one of the most populated towns on the Cape, the Nantucket Sound Community Health Care Center served hundreds of families in need every year. Patients came from as far as Wareham and Mattapoisett to receive treatment from the half dozen highly qualified professionals in residence. When outside consults were required, a network of experts from all over New England offered their services at reasonable rates. Some even worked on a pro bono basis as had been the case with Randall Landry.

No matter how hard she tried to clear her head, Abby's thoughts kept drifting back to the chilling scene on the overlook. She supposed that there were plenty of people who might have wanted to kill Randall. After all, he had been engaging in illicit affairs with married women for most of his adult life, leaving a sizeable aggregation of jilted husbands in his wake. Worse yet, he had set up a hidden camera to record footage of his trysts, some of which involved kinky activities such as BDSM. When Abby's divorce lawyers uncovered the sordid details, Randall was forced to yield to her every demand on the condition that the information never be made public. A series of clauses in their divorce agreement had legally bound her to confidentiality. Nearly seven years later, she still wasn't permitted to speak about it.

Though the particulars of Randall's exotic sexual tastes had never been leaked to the public, his affairs had been uncovered on many occasions including twice while Abby was married to him. As it turned out, Randall's preference for married women bordered on fetishism. All of the women he became involved with had been married. All of them had undergone cosmetic procedures in his clinic. Most were obscenely wealthy trophy wives bored with their matrimonial obligations. In nearly all of the cases, the husbands had the resources to exact revenge without getting their own hands dirty. Perhaps someone had finally decided to put an end to Randall.

If Randall's murder had been a contract killing, Abby wondered if it had been carried out by the man in the scarecrow costume. What was the significance of the attire? To disguise the identity of the killer or maybe to instill terror in the victim at the moment of death? If terror was the intent, why dress up as a scarecrow? Why not just toss on a vintage goalie helmet or latex William Shatner mask like the iconic serial killers in the movies? That would certainly produce the same horrifying effect.

Based on what she had seen, the CSI techs were on the right track. Even with a highly sharpened implement, it would have taken a considerable amount of strength to lop off a human head. The cuts had been made at an acute downward angle. Randall had stood over six feet so the killer would have to have been a towering figure. Her mind flashed back to the man in the costume. In the glare of her headlights, he had seemed imposingly tall. He had thrown one of his hands up to shield his masked face and his features had been completely obscured. Given one fleeting glance, all she could say for certain is that he was a vertically endowed male. Not much to go on.

The bleat of a car horn jolted her out of her contemplation. She had exited 6A at Sandwich Road and was idling at a stop sign preparing to turn off onto Maritime Lane where her housing complex was located. She had dressed hurriedly on her way to the crime scene earlier and decided it would diminish her professional image if she showed up at the clinic in a hoodie and jogging pants. Behind her, a man in a silver Audi was waving his arms and shouting. She couldn't hear what he was saying, but based on his angry gestures, she assumed he was in a hell-fired hurry. She offered an apologetic wave then turned left onto her street.

Comprised entirely of newly constructed townhouses, the complex was situated in a cul-de-sac lined with symmetrical rows of scrub pines. Behind the townhouses lay a Conrail route that traversed the entire length of the Cape Cod Canal. Had she known she'd be hearing train whistles in the middle of the night, she might have chosen another setting. Still, the place was in pristine condition and the view from her bedroom window was picturesque.

As she approached her driveway, she noticed a black SUV parked at the curb next door. There was a man on the passenger side of the vehicle wearing a knitted Patriots cap and oversized sunglasses, odd considering that it was completely overcast with unseasonably high temperatures. Last night's cold front had moved rapidly through, leaving balmy air in its wake. The weatherman on WCRB had called it "Indian Summer." Assessing the particulars, Abby observed that the man in the SUV was pointing a cell phone in the direction of her townhouse and taking pictures.

What the hell?

She slowed her vehicle hoping to get a better look, but the man spotted her from a considerable distance. His face wore a startled expression as he scrambled clumsily to the driver's side. By the time Abby reached the curb where the SUV had been parked, it was tearing swiftly around the cul-de-sac on its way out of the complex. This led her to an unsettling conclusion.

She was being watched.

10

Burroughs was finishing the last bite of an English muffin when he heard the Dragnet theme. He wondered why cell phones only seemed to ring at inconvenient times. He supposed that the technology had made life easier for millions of folks, but there were particular moments he felt should be left undisturbed. For instance, he wondered why anyone strolling along the Cape Cod National Seashore would disrupt the tranquil beauty of the surroundings by accepting a phone call. Pandemic reliance on technology in the modern world had served to disconnect many people from life's little wonders. How sad, he thought. Wiping his hands on a dish towel, he pulled the phone from his shirt pocket. He was still chewing when he answered.

"Hello. This is Thom Burroughs."

Carlson's laconic voice instantly grated on his nerves.

"Hey, Chief, I spoke to Mayor Jerzowicz a short while ago. I wanted to confirm that we're on for an 11:30 press conference at the Sandwich Town Hall. Have you ever handled anything like this?"

"Yeah, but on a smaller scale. I'm not sure which news stations the Mayor's office has reached out to, but I imagine it'll be a bit of a zoo."

"You can count on that," Carlson assured Burroughs. "The Mayor will offer a few remarks before you make your official statement. I'll handle the Q & A after that."

"Okay. I assume we'll be releasing the identity of the victim."

"Yup. If anything, putting a name out there might bring some people forward with information."

"It's liable to bring a few crackpots out of the woodwork as well," Burroughs quipped.

"I'm sure you've dealt with that before."

Burroughs couldn't tell if it was intended as an insult so he ignored the remark. "Speaking of information," he said, "I checked the local bar scene. There were no Halloween parties going on last night, at least none that were openly advertised to the general public."

"That's what I figured," Carlson replied matter of factly. "We're still waiting for those costume shops to open up, but I assume that'll be a dead end, too. There was one thing we found at the crime scene I forgot to tell you about, though."

Burroughs was intrigued. "Oh? What's that?"

"A piece of dried fruit. We found it near those motorcycle tracks at the edge of the marsh. It turned out to be an apricot. We think maybe the guy on the bike dropped it. My techs are checking it for DNA as we speak."

"It must be nice to have all those tools at your disposal," Burroughs said enviously.

"Yeah, we've got everything but the kitchen sink here. Well, I gotta run. We'll be seeing each other again in a few hours."

With that, Carlson hung up. Burroughs wondered why some people refused to say *goodbye* when a given situation called for it. In Carlson's case, it came off as a calculated refusal to extend the proper courtesy. He found it maddeningly frustrating.

As soon as he snapped his phone shut, it rang again. It was Annie from the station.

"Hey, Chief, sorry to bother you, but I just got a call from Marianne out at the Crow Farm. Apparently, there's been some vandalism."

Burroughs knew Marianne Crow well. He purchased fresh vegetables from her stand several times a week during the summer months. They had a decent variety of garden plants as well. Most of the annuals in his flower beds had come from there.

"Okay. What's Viscoli doing?"

"He's on traffic duty."

"What about Reynolds?"

"He finished up at the gas station and is handling a noise complaint."

Burroughs was running out of names.

"How about Fletcher?"

"He left at seven. He's on nights this week."

Burroughs rubbed his forehead. He could feel the warning signs of an impending headache. Budget cuts in the offseason left him with a skeleton crew most days. It could be a major inconvenience at times. "Okay, I'll talk to Marianne. I was going to work on my statement for the press conference, but I suppose I can do that after."

"You sure, Chief? I can send Reynolds along when he finishes up."

"No worries, Annie. I'll handle it. You got anything else for me?"

"Nope. But it's still early yet."

"Right. Well, keep me posted."

"I will, Chief. Bye for now."

"Bye, Annie."

11

The Crow Farm was located at the base of a small hill directly off of 6A. The forty acre homestead had been in business since 1916. It was a popular stop among locals and weekenders. The stand itself was a small cottage that had housed itinerant seasonal workers back in the day. It was full of all kinds of treasures—fresh eggs, local honey, assorted pies. Currently, there was a colorful variety of pumpkins and gourds to choose from. When the growing season was over, the farm would switch over to Christmas tree sales until the arrival of the holidays.

The store had just opened when Burroughs arrived. Marianne Crow was arranging a display filled with cider and baked goods. The enticing smell of fresh apple pie permeated the air, making Burroughs hungry. Marianne was a slender woman with graying hair and a pleasant face. She greeted him warmly as he walked in.

"Thom, how are you?"

"Fine. Yourself?"

"I didn't expect anyone to get here so quickly," she said. "I hope Annie didn't tell you it was some kind of emergency."

"She didn't specify," he said. "Smells great in here. Did those pies come fresh from the oven?"

"Yeah, Audrey's in the back working on a batch of blueberry ones. Did you want to say hello?"

"I'd love to Marianne, but my schedule's kind of full today."

"I understand," she acknowledged politely. "Well, it's nice of you to come right off, but like I said, this definitely could have waited until later."

"Annie told me there was some vandalism."

"Yeah, Halloween's right around the corner, you know."

"So you're assuming it was kids?"

"It had to have been," Marianne said. "Who else would want to steal our scarecrow?"

Burroughs felt a cold pang of dread in the pit of his stomach. "Where was the scarecrow located?" He inquired.

"Considering the line of work you're in, I'm surprised you've never noticed. It's been out near the road since August."

"That's right, of course," Thom said, feeling a bit foolish. He remembered something else about the scarecrow that made his heart race.

It had been holding a sickle.

12

Abby had finally stopped worrying about the man in the SUV by the time she walked through the doors of the clinic. She had dressed smartly in a navy blue blazer with a silk blouse and matching skirt, a far cry from the royal blue cargo pants and matching button up shirts that comprised her standard work uniform. Abby was aware that she cleaned up nicely and enjoyed dressing up. But she had always been more at ease in casual attire. She greatly preferred running shoes to the uncomfortable pumps she was currently wearing.

She padded across the carpeted waiting room to the receptionist's desk which was separated from the public by a pair of sliding glass windows. It was just a little after 9:00 and the clinic was already busy. A morbidly obese woman in a faded flower-print Mumu was hooked to a tank of oxygen. A teenage mother and her toddler son were assembling a puzzle. In the far corner of the lobby, an emaciated elderly man in a stained white tank top was fast asleep in his chair. These were the individuals the clinic catered to—people of lower socioeconomic status who couldn't afford proper medical treatment elsewhere. To the American health care system, they were the wretched refuse. To Abby, they were the demographic most in need.

The receptionist, a perky young brunette named Victoria Garrett, recognized Abby immediately and buzzed her through the door. The clinic got its fair share of drug-seeking addicts and security measures, though regrettable, were necessary. When Abby entered the office, Victoria offered her a bright smile and stood to administer a hug.

"Abby. I haven't seen you in almost a month. How have you been?"

"I'm good," Abby said, returning the friendly gesture. "I've been meaning to stop by, but something always comes up it seems. How are the little ones?"

Abby was referring to Victoria's two kids, Evan and Kayla. They were both of middle school age.

"They're great. Evan just signed up for wrestling and Kayla started taking piano lessons. She's actually pretty good at it."

"How nice," Abby remarked genially, maintaining a sincere smile. "I'll bet they're growing like weeds."

"They are," Victoria assured her. "I'd bore you with pictures but I'm sure you're pretty busy. I'll let Kelley know that you're here. She's down in her office. Thursday is her paperwork day."

Kelley Masden was the Chief Physician and Managing Director of the clinic. Abby had hand-picked her from a long list of qualified candidates. What set her apart in Abby's opinion was her passion for the work. She really believed in what they were doing here and she maintained excellent rapport with potential benefactors.

"Maybe I'll just walk down and surprise her," Abby suggested.

"Yeah, why don't you?" Victoria said enthusiastically. "I'm sure she won't mind."

"Thanks, Victoria. So nice to see you."

"Yeah. Same here. Take care of yourself."

Abby exited the reception area and entered a long hallway lined with examination rooms. It was brightly lit and painted a sterile white. There was a supply closet at the end of the corridor. From there, the hall took a ninety-degree turn, leading to a row of physicians' offices. Kelley's office was the last one on the right. The door was ajar and Abby found the Director sitting at her desk examining a large batch of medical invoices.

Responding to Abby's polite knock, Kelley looked up from her desk and brightened instantly. "Abby! What a nice surprise. Did you come to rescue me from all this paperwork?"

"I'd love to," Abby joked. "Where should we go, out to the Vineyard for the day?"

"Sounds good to me. It'd be a shame to waste this weather. Can you believe how warm it is outside?"

"I know," said Abby. "They're calling it Indian summer."

"Whatever it is, I want more of it," Kelley replied, gesturing toward one of the chairs stationed in front of her desk. "C'mon in and have a seat."

"No, it's okay," Abby responded courteously. "There's no specific reason for my visit. I'm just in between cases right now and thought I'd drop by to say hello. I don't want to keep you from anything important."

"Don't be silly. I was going to have a cup of coffee, anyway. These invoices can wait until after. Take a walk with me."

"Well, all right. I could use a cup."

Abby followed Kelley to the break room which was located at the opposite end of the hall. The coffee maker on the counter was still gurgling, having recently produced a fresh batch. The aroma filled the room. Abby had always loved the smell of coffee. It inexplicably reminded her of lazy weekend mornings during her undergraduate days at Gordon College.

Kelley grabbed a pair of cups from a nearby cabinet and filled them, leaving enough room for cream. "You like yours light and sweet, right?"

"It's amazing how you retain so many small details," Abby said appreciatively. "I guess that's one of the qualities that make you a great director."

"It's nice of you to say so," Kelley replied, stirring their coffees. "But some days I feel like I'm just treading water."

"I'm sure it can be overwhelming at times," Abby sympathized. "Remember, I'm never more than a phone call away."

"Thanks. I do appreciate that. Did you hear about the fundraiser for the Cape Cod Hospital last night?"

"What fund raiser?"

"Over at the big convention hall in Harwich," Kelley said, handing Abby a steaming mug. "It was a costume party."

Abby was so startled by the comment she spilled half of her coffee on the linoleum floor.

13

Having concluded his business at the Crow Farm, Burroughs climbed into his Jeep and headed back to the station. The morning traffic had thinned out dramatically, making it an easy commute. He cautioned himself not to put undue emphasis on this latest piece of information. A missing scarecrow from a farm stand located less than three miles from the Landry murder site was an intriguing scenario for certain, but it could still turn out to be nothing more than an amazing coincidence. Some of the kids in Sandwich were accomplished pranksters. The gristmill duck gag was just a small sampling of the shenanigans that had taken place last Halloween. A statue of Paul Revere stolen from a local miniature golf course had been found on the shoulder of Route 6 just outside Provincetown. It had been decked out in lingerie from Victoria's Secret. The culprits were apprehended after a series of photos chronicling the midnight rider's journey had been posted on Facebook. The lengths that some teenagers would go to often amazed Burroughs. But on the other hand, the missing scarecrow could turn out to be a solid lead. Having obtained a full description from Marianne Crow, he intended to question Abby again about the one she had seen in the parking lot last night. If the two accounts matched, then perhaps they were onto something big.

Upon arriving at the station, Burroughs dialed Abby's cell phone number from memory. She answered on the second ring.

"Wow, Thom, that's amazing. I was just going to call you."

"Really? They say great minds think alike. What's up?"

"There've been some new developments on my end."

"Mine, too," Thom told her. "Why don't you go first?"

"Okay," she said, the excitement in her voice evident. "I just met with Kelley Masden, she's the managing director at the clinic. She told me about a fundraiser that was held at a banquet hall in Harwich to benefit the Cape Cod Hospital. Get this: It was a costume party."

"Interesting," Thom commented.

"Kelley doesn't work on fundraising for the hospital, but she knows people that do. She thought she might be able to get her hands on a copy of the guest list."

"Excellent. That would certainly help us out. I hope you didn't tell her much about the case."

"No. I figured I should wait until after the press conference. When *is* that, anyway?"

"Eleven-thirty. I need to work on my statement, but I wanted to call you first. Anything else worth reporting?"

Abby considered telling Thom about the SUV parked outside her townhouse earlier but didn't want to come off as neurotic or paranoid. Despite the man's suspicious behavior, there could be a perfectly benign explanation for his presence. Maybe he worked for National Grid or Pine Vista, though she was pretty sure the vehicle would have been marked with a company logo. Whatever the case, there was no need to mention it to Thom unless she encountered the man again.

"Nope, that's about it," she answered, avoiding the subject. "So what's *your* big news?"

"I got called to the Crow Farm out on 6A. It's fairly close to the murder scene. Turns out that their scarecrow was stolen at some point last night."

Abby felt a chill. "You're kidding."

"Nope. Guess what the scarecrow was holding?"

"I'll bet it was something sharp," she said soberly.

"Yup, a sickle. Was the man at the overlook wearing a green flannel work shirt under bib coveralls?"

She called up the image in her mind. The glimpse she had gotten of the figure was so brief. But there had been enough time to take in a few small details. "Yes," she answered. "He had a red bandana. It was tucked into his shirt like a scarf. The pants were way too short for him. There was hay sticking out of the cuffs and he had patches all over. One of them was a peace sign."

"Abby, you just described the Crow Farm scarecrow to a T," Thom said dramatically. "Was he wearing a mask?"

"Yeah, but I didn't get a good look at it. He put his hand up to cover his face."

"I see. Well, Marianne said her scarecrow had a burlap mask with a smiley face painted on it."

Abby thought about the party in Harwich last night and suddenly wondered how the two events were connected. Why would someone steal a scarecrow from a farm stand to wear as a costume to a $150 per plate fundraiser? It didn't make sense. She voiced her concern to Thom.

"Maybe the guy wasn't a benefactor. Maybe he worked at the banquet hall. Or maybe the fundraiser has nothing to do with Randall's murder. Whatever the case, we have a lot more information than we did at 4 a.m. this morning. As soon as we get this press conference out of the way, we can move on to the business of detecting."

"You said 'we.' I thought I wasn't allowed in this investigation," she commented sarcastically.

"You're one of the smartest people I know. You didn't think I was going to solve this thing all by myself did you?"

"Thom, are you suggesting we violate procedural policy?"

"Yeah, something like that."

"I love it when you go all maverick," she joked.

"Yeah, that's me," he deadpanned. "But you'll have to operate behind the scenes. Even mavericks have their limits."

"I understand. It'll be our little secret."

"I like the sound of that."

"Me, too."

There was a brief pause as Thom contemplated how very much he enjoyed working with Abby.

"Well, you should probably go write that statement of yours, Chief," Abby said. "Let me know how it turns out."

"I will. Bye, Abby."

"Bye, Thom."

14

They came from all over New England, filling the Sandwich Town Hall as if it were an intimate tour stop for a popular rock band. They came armed with quips and queries and insinuations. They came in droves despite the fact that the Sandwich Police force was too small to handle their numbers. They arrived in the hope of obtaining enough squalid details about millionaire playboy Randall Landry to satisfy their inquisitive followers.

It began with a few awkward introductory statements from Mayor Joseph Jerzowicz, a balding middle age buffoon with sausage fingers. The Jerzowicz family had presided over Sandwich for so long, older folks in the community may not even have realized they were voting for the youngest grandson when they pulled the lever on Election Day. After some hastily prepared words about the competence of local officers working in conjunction with the State CSI unit, it was Burroughs' turn in the spotlight.

There were clicks and pings and flashes. There was the collective groan of folding chairs as the army of reporters shifted restlessly in their seats. And for the first time during his tenure as Chief of the Sandwich Police Department, Burroughs felt deeply uncomfortable. He fumbled through his part of the script, all three hundred and seventy-eight words of it, then yielded the microphone to Carlson.

Carlson's cool demeanor did nothing to deter the barrage of questions and interjections. He fought many of them off with a canned "no comment" remark. He offered up a sparse assortment of facts, most of which had already been covered in Burroughs' brief dialog. He assured them that the investigation was just beginning and the media would be informed of developments as they occurred. He handled it like a veteran of such proceedings.

Burroughs was not surprised when Abby's name surfaced a mere five minutes into the Q & A session. A reporter from WCVB TV in Boston wanted to know if she was a suspect. A guy from WRKO Radio quickly followed up, wondering if she had been notified and, if so, what her reaction had been. Burroughs resisted the powerful urge to club him over the head with a boom mic. Carlson asserted that Doctor Abigail Rhodes was not under investigation at the present. This prompted a few more inquiries, but the line of questioning quickly ran out of steam.

When the conference was finished, it took two of Burroughs' men and a gaggle of state troopers to deal with the snarl of traffic which was clustered all over town and choking most of the side streets. A small throng of reporters lingered to press Carlson and Burroughs for more information as they exited the antiquated hall together. Carlson dismissed them with a smug look and a sanctimonious wave of his hand. "At this point, you know as much as we do," he huffed. "Why don't we all just pick up our toys and go home like good boys and girls?"

Since there had been little time to exchange information before the conference, Carlson invited Burroughs to sit in his vehicle and chat. It was a department-issued Chevy Yukon with a cavernous interior and all the latest toys. Burroughs considered the perks of being a crime scene investigator at the state level. With a small fraction of Carlson's budget, he could dole out much-needed raises to everyone on his force. He understood that state forensic units dealt with more pressing matters than the ones that typically surfaced in Sandwich, but it still didn't seem fair that Carlson was driving a car fresh off the lot while his own men were patrolling the streets in units that were nearly ten years old. It was just another one of life's injustices, he supposed.

Burroughs told Carlson about the missing scarecrow and the costume party in Harwich. He offered to produce a copy of the guest list and weed out potential suspects. Carlson listened with a flat expression. He was snacking on a Freihofer's donut. White powder was falling all over his shirt and had gathered at the corners of his mouth.

"That's a generous offer, but I think we'll handle the guest list. So, you said this scarecrow was stolen from a local farm stand. Do you know when?"

"The place closes at five-thirty," Burroughs answered. "Apparently, it was still there when the owner packed up for the night."

"And what time was the costume party?"

"Don't know, but I can easily find out."

"No need to trouble yourself. I already got a couple of guys working on leads," Carlson said with his mouth full. "My forensic team found large deposits of iron oxide in the wound indicating that the murder weapon was old and rusty. That lends a little more credence to the scarecrow connection. Did you check with Doctor Rhodes to see if her description matched the one from the farm?"

"I did and yes, she pretty much confirmed it."

"Hmm," said Carlson, licking his lips. "So the guy she saw in the parking lot might have been the killer after all. I was a little skeptical at first."

"Yeah, me, too," Burroughs admitted. "Who goes around murdering people in a scarecrow costume?"

"Don't know. Maybe someone trying to throw us off track."

"What do you mean?"

"Everyone in New England knows about Randall Landry. High profile murders are rarely the work of random serial killers. And the location was pretty ideal. So the whole scarecrow thing seems kind of hokey ... like it was staged."

"I agree. But by who?"

"How well do you know Doctor Rhodes, Chief?"

Burroughs instantly felt defensive but made a concerted effort to hide it. If he overreacted, he was liable to find himself out of the loop. "Pretty well, I guess," he said evenly. "I mean, I've been working with her for about six years now."

"You ever see her outside of work?"

"Not much."

"Does she ever talk about her ex-husband?"

"Rarely. She's very professional."

"Yeah, I get that. But she *has* mentioned him?"

"It would be impossible not to. Randall was the New England equivalent of Hugh Hefner and he abused her both physically and mentally."

"Right," Carlson pressed. "So, what kind of stuff has she said about him?"

"Nothing vindictive if that's what you're driving at. It's pretty obvious that she's moved on with her life."

"So how did she end up at a secluded overlook with him last night?"

Burroughs despised the fact that Carlson was trying to instill doubt in him. He considered himself an impeccable judge of character and he liked Abby very much. He couldn't deny that there were details of her life he wasn't privy to. But he was certain he would have noticed if there was anything shady about her.

"We know she's not our killer because the deathblow was delivered by someone much taller and stronger," Carlson went on. "But who's to say she didn't hire someone to do it? Isn't it awfully convenient that she was leaving the scene just as the person in the scarecrow costume was arriving?"

"I see your point," Burroughs conceded, playing along. "But according to her, it was Randall's idea to go to the overlook. The place is pretty secluded and there were no witnesses. Why would she admit to having been there if she had something to hide?"

"Good question," Carlson remarked. "You've been offering to help with this investigation. Well, here's your chance. I need you to keep an eye on Doctor Rhodes. The two of you are friends, I presume?"

"Sure," Burroughs fumbled, uncertain as to how their relationship could be defined. "We get along pretty well I guess."

"Good. I need you to stay in close contact with her over the next few days. Keep track of her comings and goings. If you notice anything hinky, let me know."

Burroughs considered telling the lieutenant where to get off but reminded himself again that it would lead to his immediate dismissal from the case. "So, you consider Doctor Rhodes a suspect?" He inquired cautiously.

"Not necessarily," Carlson said, wiping the white powder from his mouth. It left a stain on his sleeve. "At the moment, I'm willing to take your word for it that she's on the level. But let's not be stupid here. The whole story is highly suspicious and it's best we keep an eye on her for a while. I believe you're the man for the assignment."

"Right," Burroughs said through clenched teeth.

The thought of Abby hiring someone to kill Randall was preposterous to Burroughs. She had worked hard to reinvent herself after Randall had put her in the hospital and she had used a sizeable portion of her divorce settlement to give back to the community. Why jeopardize all she had accomplished with a senseless act of revenge?

"No, problem, Lieutenant," said the Chief, his voice sounding cool and collected. "I'm happy to help in any way I can."

"Good," Carlson responded dismissively. "So where can I get a good cup of chowder around here?"

Abby knew the press conference was over when the first news truck arrived in front of her townhouse. It was followed by a wake of fellow vultures. By 12:30, the protracted line of vehicles representing every imaginable news medium had completely clogged the cul-de-sac around her complex.

Pine Vista was not technically a gated community, so as long as the legion of journalists behaved themselves, they had every right to be here. This was worse than Abby had anticipated. The highly publicized divorce followed by the opening of the clinic in Hyannis had thrust her into the regional spotlight. She tried her best to be accommodating at first. But when the reporters started following her to work and camping out on her property, she had asked for the protection of the Sandwich police. Realizing that her affiliation with the clinic had actually become a detriment to its daily operations, she had taken the coroner's job and moved from Sandwich to Yarmouth, later ending up in Bourne. But that was six years ago. How on Earth was she still considered newsworthy?

Abby ambled to the living room and tuned the television to Channel 5 out of Boston. She found it difficult to wrap her head around what she was seeing.

A live feed of her front door.

Damn, she thought.

She grabbed the remote and turned up the sound. It was a habit of hers to read and watch TV at the same time. She had been a multi-tasker since college. When the dialog became too distracting, she often muted the offending program. Apparently, that had been the case the last time she had sat in front of the television.

An attractive female reporter was standing near the edge of her front lawn regurgitating details from the recently concluded press conference.

"… police have confirmed that Landry was murdered, but refused to release any further information. Landry's ex-wife, Abby Rhodes, who opened a public health care center in Hyannis with the funds she received from the couple's bitter divorce, has not been cited as a suspect. We're outside her house right now hoping to get a statement."

Parasites, Abby thought. This was intolerable. Some of the news teams had already overstepped their boundaries, setting up equipment right on her lawn. How was she supposed to get in and out of the house without being accosted? Slipping out the back door provided no solution. She would still need to get to her car, which was parked in the driveway out front. Stepping outside and facing reporters was ill-advised. That would only lead to more questions and more intrusions.

There was no escape.

For the time being, she was trapped in her own home.

16

Burroughs was attempting to catch up on some obligatory paperwork when Annie rapped on his office door. She was a big woman in her mid-thirties with dark hair that was always pulled up in a tidy bun. Her eyes were a sparkling shade of emerald green, but aside from that, she had a forgettable face. She always smelled of cinnamon, though Burroughs had never noticed her chewing gum or sucking on breath mints. It was a little odd.

"Chief, you should come take a look at what's on TV," she said in her nasally voice.

"Annie, are you still here?"

"Yeah, my shift started at four. Nadia was supposed to be here, but she called to say she's running a little late."

"Oh. Do you need to get going?"

"No, it's all right. I can hang around for a little while," She assured him.

"Thanks," he said, relieved that she didn't have anything pressing going on outside of work. That would temporarily leave him without a dispatcher.

"You're really going to want to check out the news," she said.

"Are they running the story already?"

"Oh, Yeah. They've launched a full-scale assault on Doctor Rhodes' house."

That definitely got Burroughs' attention. He immediately abandoned his paperwork and followed Annie into the empty lobby where the dispatcher's station was located. A row of plastic chairs faced a wall-mounted television and soda machine. Burroughs had no idea whose lame-brained decision it had been to offer Coke products only. He had always been a Pepsi man, himself.

On the TV, FOX 25 had a male reporter stationed outside a modern-looking housing complex. The camera panned left along the access road, revealing a solid wall of news trucks. A graphic on the bottom of the screen read: *Bourne, Massachusetts.* Thom had actually never been to Abby's home and didn't recognize the setting.

"How do you know it's her house?"

"The guy on the news said it was," Annie informed him.

"Damn," he muttered.

He headed back toward his office, pulling his cell phone out on the way. Abby sounded tired and frustrated when she answered his call.

"I see you've got company," he said.

"Yup. I really wish I was less popular sometimes."

"I don't blame you," he commented. "So, what's your plan?"

"Can you send a cruiser out here to get me?"

He considered the possibility. "Well, it's technically out of our jurisdiction," he told her.

"You're kidding right?"

"Nope. Chief Grimsley from the Bourne precinct is a bit of a stickler about details, I'm afraid."

"So you guys always play by the rules?"

"Not me. My policy is to grab the damsel first and deal with the fallout later. What's your address?"

"118 Maritime Lane."

"I'll be there in about fifteen minutes. Keep an eye out for me. Do you have anyone you can stay with for a day or two until this blows over?"

She contemplated the question. Her parents were in Florida. Most of her other acquaintances were strictly professional. *Some life I'm* leading here, she thought to herself. Trust issues had led her to a solitary existence.

"Not really," she told Thom. "But I'm sure I can find a hotel somewhere."

"My guest house is available. It's nothing fancy, but you're welcome to it."

"Wouldn't that be an imposition?" She said mildly.

"Not at all," he insisted. "I won't even charge you as long as you promise to eat some of my food. I get tired of cooking for just myself."

"Fair enough," she agreed.

"Okay, Doc, it tight. Help is on the way."

***

After Thom hung up Abby threw some clothes together in a gym bag. Nothing too frilly. She didn't want him to get the mistaken impression that she was dressing up for him. She had always been a fairly low maintenance gal so the number of personal products she added to the mix was marginal. She had just finished packing when her cell phone chirped again.

She hoped the reporters hadn't gotten a hold of her number. She had paid for a private listing, although she doubted that would stop someone even mildly ambitious from gaining access to it. Nowadays, there were plenty of online sources that furnished private information for a fee. When Abby saw the number of the caller, her heart literally skipped a beat. It was Randall's father.

Just what I need right now, another confrontation, she thought.

She answered nervously, her voice cracking on the last syllable.

Douglas Landry's voice had a ridiculous affectation. Though he had been born in Dover, Massachusetts, he sounded vaguely British. His pretentious mannerisms reminded Abby of the Thurston Howell III character from the classic *Gilligan's Island* TV show. Though Douglas considered himself to be a pillar of the community, he more closely resembled a cartoon character in Abby's opinion.

"I know what you did and you're not going to get away with it," he said venomously.

"Well, hello to you, too, Douglas."

"Don't presume to be innocent, you gold-digging bitch. You've been extorting money out of my son for years."

Abby had no idea what he was referring to. By her own choice, the divorce settlement had come in a lump sum. She had wanted nothing to do with monthly alimony payments since that would have tied her to Randall.

"I'm sure you're quite upset about your son, but I'm at a complete loss here," she told the doctor. "What exactly are you talking about?"

"You've finally gone too far," he shouted. "I spoke to Lieutenant Carlson. You're going to get exactly what you deserve. It's over now, do you hear me?"

And with that, he hung up on her.

Boy, she thought. What a strange and horrible day this was turning out to be.

17

Thom's guest house was not much bigger than a standard room at a major hotel chain. There was a galley kitchen, a bathroom, and a small sitting area. But what it lacked in square footage it made up for with charm. The walls were brightly painted and adorned with the works of local artists. Every flat surface had something interesting placed on it. There were decoy ducks, antique lanterns, and assorted pieces of nautically themed bric-a-brac. A window in the sitting area looked out on the beautifully landscaped yard. Like every other glimpse she had gotten into Thom's life, the place confirmed the fact that he had impeccable taste.

The sitting area was furnished with a futon and an old-fashioned rocker. She set her gym bag on the floor next to the futon and took a seat while Thom remained standing by the door.

"Like I said, it's not much," he told her humbly, "but it's a lot more peaceful than Pine Vista at the moment."

"No doubt," she agreed. "Thanks so much for rescuing me, Thom. That seems to be an ongoing theme in my life."

He had arrived in a Sandwich squad car with the lights flashing. A horde of reporters had encircled him as he made his way up the sidewalk. He had shooed them away politely, telling them that he was "conducting official police business." Abby had been peppered with questions as she climbed into the cruiser. More than one reporter assumed that she was now a prime suspect. The ride back to Sandwich had been a quiet one, neither of them trying to manufacture unnecessary talk. The collective experience was beginning to take a serious toll on Abby's nerves.

"Well, I should give you some space," Thom said. "I've got to get back to the station. If you need anything, call."

"I will," she said, offering a tired smile. "I feel sort of helpless. I'm not used to having people take care of me like this."

"It's no trouble, Abby ... really," he assured her. "This is what I do."

"Yeah," she said. "You seem to have a knack for it."

She could tell he was flattered by the remark. He nodded once and opened the door. Before he left, she added a bit timidly, "Maybe I'll take you up on that dinner offer later. I mean, if you're still interested."

"Sure," he said. "Do you like seafood?"

"I live on Cape Cod," she confirmed. "That's no coincidence."

"Good. I've got a fresh batch of bay scallops. I could throw together a mushroom risotto to go with it."

Her stomach grumbled spontaneously. "That sounds fantastic."

"We can talk a little shop over dinner," he suggested.

"Yeah," she agreed. "There are a couple of things I should probably discuss with you at some point."

"Okay. I usually wrap up around five unless something big comes up. On a day like today, you never know."

"Tell me about it," she said cynically.

"If you get hungry before then, the key to the main house is under the mat in the carport."

"That's not terribly imaginative, Chief," she teased. "That's the first place I would have looked."

He chuckled. "It's pretty quiet on the marsh. Most criminal types don't even realize there are houses out here."

"Well, that's a relief," she said.

There was a short pause as the conversation reached a natural stopping point. Thom was still hovering in the doorway, waiting for a cue.

"You better run," she urged him. "Lots of stuff going on."

"Okay, let's shoot for around 6:00 for dinner. I'll call you if I get sidetracked at work."

"Sounds good. Bye, Chief."

"Bye, Abby. Try to relax a little."

"I will. Thanks again for everything."

"You're very welcome."

And with that, he was out the door.

18

Annie was gone by the time Burroughs returned to the station. Her replacement, Nadia Welles, was glued to the television. She had switched it from FOX to NBC. A talk show doctor was rambling on about the potential dangers of various skin products.

"How's it going, Nadia?"

"Not bad, Chief."

Nadia was an attractive redhead in her early forties. Her husband operated a small marina in Wellfleet where many of the Cape's summer inhabitants kept their boats moored during the offseason. Nadia had no interest in boats or the ocean in general, odd considering her geographical location, and had applied for the dispatcher's position in the hope of avoiding a career of perceived drudgery alongside her husband. She was smart, personable and highly efficient. Definitely one of Thom's better hires.

"Anything new?" He asked her.

"Yeah. Reporters have been swarming the marsh overlook. The state CSI unit put up yellow tape, but the trooper on guard is having a helluva of a time preserving the integrity of the crime scene. Sergeant Strack called from Bourne. He was wondering if we could put one of our own guys out there."

"Yeah, like we've got bodies to spare," Burroughs griped. "I thought the CSI crew was finished."

"According to Strack, they haven't received clearance to open the site to the public yet."

"All right. I'll speak to Lieutenant Carlson and find out what the holdup is. Anything else going on?"

"Yup. The Mayor called. He wants you to do something about the reporters snooping around town." She smiled. "His words ... not mine."

"Well, he should have thought about that before he called a press conference," Burroughs said, his tone a bit peevish. "Can you get a hold of him for me and tell him we're handling it?"

"No problem, Chief."

"Thanks."

Burroughs headed back to his office. While he had gotten into a habit of using his cell phone, it seemed wasteful somehow not to use the landlines once in a while. He pulled Carlson's business card from his wallet and dialed the number from his desk phone. It was a cordless model with a digital answering machine. In the relatively short time it had taken to rescue Abby, the machine had recorded seven new messages. Good times, he thought.

Carlson sounded impatient and irritable as usual when he answered.

"Carlson here."

"Hello, Lieutenant, it's Thom Burroughs."

There was an inordinate pause. Burroughs could hear road noise.

"What can I do for you, Chief?"

"I was wondering when you were going to clear that crime scene for public use."

"You in a hurry or something?"

"Not particularly, but there's a trooper out there trying to fend off an army of reporters. The Bourne division called us for backup and I don't have too many officers to go around. Seems a little unfair to leave us all hanging."

Carlson grunted. "Yeah, we've got everything we need I guess. Tell them to pack it in."

"All right, will do."

"Hey, Chief, while I got you on the line, there's something I want to talk about. In fact, I was going to get in touch with you anyway."

"What's up?"

"When I spoke to the victim's next of kin, he didn't have anything nice to say about you or Doctor Rhodes."

"I assume you're talking about Douglas Landry," said Burroughs. "I told you there was no love lost between us. Abby got half of everything Randall owned in the divorce. Douglas threatened to sue me when I decked his son a few years ago."

"Right," Carlson acknowledged. "I remember you mentioning that. But now I'm wondering if there's a little more to the story."

Burroughs wasn't sure what Carlson was driving at, but he was relatively certain he wasn't going to like it.

"It seems that the good doctor has this crazy idea about you and his former daughter-in-law."

"Really," Burroughs said acidly. "I can't wait to hear this."

"He believes the two of you have been blackmailing his son. He says you bankrupted the poor man."

Carlson's voice was dripping with sarcasm. Burroughs came to the abrupt conclusion that he didn't like the lieutenant much.

"Blackmail? That's ridiculous. What would Abby and I have to hold over Randall's head?"

"He didn't specify. But he did say it had something to do with the divorce settlement. Does that set off any bells for you?"

"No. Why would it?"

"Maybe you need to have a chat with Doctor Rhodes, Chief. Have you checked in with her lately?"

"Yeah. I picked her up from her townhouse in Bourne. There were reporters crawling all over the place."

"She staying with friends?"

Burroughs felt a strong protective impulse. He decided it was best not to disclose Abby's current location. If Carlson had any doubts about what the two of them might be up to, that information might make their activities appear even more suspicious.

"Yeah," he answered stiffly.

"See if you can get anything out of her. It might help establish a motive."

"Okay, I will."

"Oh, remember that piece of dried fruit we found?"

"Yup. Near the motorcycle tracks."

"My guys were able to get enough DNA off it to run some tests. Turns out the DNA doesn't match anyone in the system—so far, anyway. We're still running it. The motorcycle tracks didn't help much. The same treads can be found on any number of racing bikes. We assume it was a rice-burner. Definitely wasn't a Harley."

"Well, that's something, I guess," Burroughs commented, pleased to find himself in the loop for the time being.

"Is there anything else you want to tell me, Chief?"

It sounded like a loaded question.

"Not that I can think of," Burroughs answered in a defensive tone.

"All right, then," Carlson said dubiously, ending the call.

Dammit, thought Burroughs, the man was infuriating.

19

Despite a steady torrent of phone calls, Burroughs managed to complete his paperwork and leave the station on time. On the way home, he stopped at a local package store to pick up a bottle of Pinot Grigio. He chose a top shelf brand from *J Vineyards* in California. The dry white wine would enhance the flavor of his risotto and he could serve whatever was left with dinner.

By 6:00, he was clad in an apron with his culinary skills on display to Abby. He wasn't deliberately trying to show off. Cooking was one of his favorite hobbies and he prepared elaborate meals for himself several times per week. But the presence of company added a subtle flair to his technique.

Abby sat at the breakfast bar sipping wine while Thom combined porcini mushrooms with fresh onions, herbs, and garlic from the Crow Farm. He added chicken broth, rice and wine to the mix in stages, cooking the mixture down until it had a creamy consistency. The final step of the process was to stir in parmesan cheese.

In contrast, preparing scallops was fast and easy. He melted some butter in a skillet and pan-seared them for about three minutes per side. The sugars in the shellfish had a caramelizing effect, turning them a golden brown.

"That smells delicious," Abby commented as Thom spooned ample portions of scallops onto their plates. A few scoops of risotto completed the meal.

Thom sat across from her at the breakfast bar and they ate without speaking for a few minutes, each of them savoring the flavor. Thom had tuned the radio to a classic rock station out of Hyannis.

"I swear to God," Abby said with her mouth full of food, "this is the best risotto I've ever eaten. What's your secret?"

"I'd tell you, but if I did, I'd have to kill you," Thom joked. No sooner had he spoken the words when he realized it had been an awkward statement. "Ouch," he said apologetically. "I definitely could have chosen a better cliché."

"It's okay," she told him. "Considering the line of work I'm in, it takes a lot more than that to upset me."

"Good," said Thom. "I'd hate to have you run off hungry."

"Nowhere to run right now, anyway," she replied.

"I know. That was quite a scene out at your place today."

"Yeah, but fortunately, reporters are like all other parasites. When they realize they don't have a host, they move on."

"I figure the worst of it should blow over in a day or two."

"I hope so. I feel really bad about dragging you into this."

"You didn't drag me into anything," he assured her. "This case fell into my lap. I wasn't about to leave a colleague in a tight spot and, besides, I like having you around. It gets awful quiet around here sometimes."

"I know the feeling," she said.

There was another comfortable silence as they set about the task of cleaning off their plates.

"I don't know if you're into dessert," he said after he had taken his last bite, "but I've got a couple of raspberry parfaits chilling in the fridge."

"You're a wicked man, Thom Burroughs," she needled. "You're going to make me fat."

He smiled. "I can assure you, my intentions are pure."

When she had finished the main course, Thom put her plate near the sink and replaced it with a cup of the parfait he had prepared. He had made the whipped cream from scratch and then layered it with raspberry sauce, fruit and Greek-style yogurt in an attractive swirling pattern.

"I have one confession to make," he said after he had set the glass in front of her. "I couldn't get my hands on any fresh local raspberries. These ones came from Stop & Shop."

"You hack," Abby berated him playfully, taking a bite. It was wonderful and she told him so. "While we're on the subject of confessions," she added. "I mentioned earlier that there was something I needed to talk to you about."

"Sounds serious," Thom said.

"It is," she confirmed, regretting the fact that she was about to spoil their dessert. "But never mind. It can wait until later I guess."

"No, Abby, it's fine. I want you to feel like you can talk to me about anything. If it's about the case, we need to discuss it anyway."

"Okay," she said, gathering her thoughts. "There's something I haven't been open with you about—something about Randall. But it's not because I was hiding information. It's because there was a gag order in place."

"The order was included in your divorce agreement?" he presumed.

"Yes. And now that Randall is dead, I'm wondering if I'm still legally bound to confidentiality."

Thom's brow furrowed. "Hmm, depends on the situation I guess. If it's information pertaining to a murder case, I assume there would be no breach of trust if you discussed it with investigators. But releasing details to the press might land you in some hot water."

"That's kind of what I figured. All right, then, I guess there's something you should know about Randall."

She paused, fumbling for the right words as Thom waited patiently.

"This is an embarrassing topic, so try to bear with me as I stumble through it," she began.

"It's fine," he said in a comforting tone. "Take your time."

"The night Randall put me in the hospital … it wasn't the first time he had hit me. He had a quick temper and would fly off the handle without much provocation. I'm not sure why I put up with it for so long. Maybe because I was young and green and he was the Great Randall Landry—pioneer in his field. At any rate, whenever he got violent, he was smart about not leaving bruises or marks where anyone could see them. I was ashamed of what was happening, so I kept it to myself."

She cleared her throat and stopped to collect her thoughts. There was a tired expression on her face. Thom sensed that this was a topic she had kept buried for quite some time.

"Shortly after we were married, I found out that Randall had unusual sexual appetites. He wasn't like that when we were dating. But as soon as the ring was on my finger, he started getting rough and bringing home toys to play out his fantasies—handcuffs, gags, latex outfits." Her face reddened as she disclosed this information. "I tried to go along with it, but it just didn't suit my tastes. I felt cheap and degraded. When I finally told him that, he got angry and called me a frigid bitch. He said I needed to be more adventurous or he would leave me. But I stood my ground. And that's when the affairs started."

She took a few bites of her parfait as if it would help erase the memories.

"That must have been rough on you," Thom sympathized.

"It was. I got really depressed and thought I was losing my mind. But then he did me a favor and beat me to a bloody pulp. I'm sure you remember that night. It really woke me up to the fact that I was better off without him."

In spite of the uncomfortable subject matter, Abby was clearly enjoying her dessert. She kept shoveling it in and making unconscious sounds of approval. Thom took it as a compliment.

"Before the divorce proceedings, my attorney enlisted the help of a private investigator. Randall had hired his father's lawyer, one of the best in New England, and we knew he'd be fighting tooth and nail to hang onto his assets. As it turns out, our investigator dug up all kinds of dirt that put Randall in a compromising position."

She had finished her cup of parfait and was now eye-balling Thom's. He slid it across the counter and she dug right in.

"Randall had sweet-talked some of his surgically enhanced beauties into getting kinky with him. He set up hidden cameras to secretly film his trysts," she went on.

Thom couldn't resist interrupting her here. "How kinky are we talking?"

"Soft porn mostly. Bondage … domination … girls in outfits. He liked to tie women up. He got pretty rough with some of them, but I don't think anyone was hurt. Anyway, all of them were married to rich and influential men. It was a divorce lawyer's dream. I got everything I asked for in the settlement on the condition that I never breathe a word about the videos or the physical abuse he put me through. Randall and his father had a highly successful medical practice. Obviously, it could hurt both of their careers if word got out."

It was a lot to digest, so Thom didn't respond immediately.

"What do you suppose happened to the videos?" he asked after a short pause.

"I have no idea," Abby responded. "I always assumed they were destroyed."

"Suppose they weren't. Suppose a third party got their hands on them and was using them to blackmail Randall and his father."

"Funny you should say that. I got a disturbing phone call from Douglas this morning."

"Really?"

"Yeah, it was bizarre. I haven't talked to him since the divorce. He was extremely angry—called me a gold-digging bitch and accused me of extorting money from his son. When I told him I had no idea what he was talking about, he started yelling about how I had finally gone too far. He said I was going to get what I deserved. Those were his exact words."

"Interesting," Thom said. "Apparently, he made the same accusation to Lieutenant Carlson, except he added my name to the mix. I'd love to tell you the lieutenant wasn't buying into it, but that didn't seem to be the case."

"He thinks the two of us have been blackmailing the Landry's?"

"Let's just say he hasn't ruled it out at this point."

"Thom, I got all the money anyone could hope for and then some in a lump settlement. Why would I want to do that?" Abby said defensively.

"You don't have to explain yourself to me," Thom asserted, "but blackmail is a motive for murder and that's exactly what Carlson needs to close this case."

"So you think it was a blackmailer who followed Randall out to the overlook and killed him?"

"It certainly puts things into perspective."

"But why the scarecrow costume and the sickle?" Abby wondered. "Why didn't the killer just wear a ski mask and use a gun?"

"I don't get it either," said Thom.

Abby exhaled deeply and rubbed her tired eyes. "This has been one of the most stressful days I've had in a long time."

"No kidding," said Thom. "I'm sure there'll be a few more before this is over."

He had no idea just how poignant that statement would prove to be.

Loose Ends

1

In the morning, Abby woke early. She was slightly disoriented and it took her a few seconds to remember where she was. As she looked out the window and saw shafts of light streaming into Thom's meticulously landscaped yard, the events of the past twenty-four hours came flooding back to her. Despite her current situation—the grisly death of her ex-husband, the full-scale media blitz at Pine Vista—she felt warm and safe. Nestled beneath the authentic Amish quilt Thom had provided, it occurred to her that she was relatively unfamiliar with this feeling.

Though the cuts, bruises, and breaks from Randall's savage beating had healed rather quickly, she had carried the psychological scars for years. Even now, she had difficulty trusting people. After the divorce, she had thrown herself into work to avoid consciously dealing with issues of guilt, shame, and worthlessness. Her mother had talked her into seeing a therapist, but Abby had never put much faith in the profession and the sessions had ended abruptly without tangible results. As the clinic in Hyannis began to take shape, she felt herself being reborn in a sense. She was redefining who she was and her place in the world. Instead of being a victim, she was becoming a savior and protector of *other* victims. But the unsolicited media attention had driven her back into the shadows. It seemed that no matter where she was or what she was doing, she couldn't shake her association with the officious Randall Landry.

For the past several years, Abby had been working as a Barnstable County coroner. Unlike other areas of Massachusetts, it was an appointed position as opposed to an elected one. There were fifteen towns in the county, which consisted entirely of Cape Cod and the associated islands, served by three doctors. Abby's jurisdiction included Bourne, Sandwich, Mashpee, and Falmouth along with Nantucket and Martha's Vineyard. The terms "coroner" and "medical examiner" were interchangeable. She performed autopsies and ran forensic tests when necessary while additionally making arrangements with funeral directors and serving as a primary contact to grieving families. During the summer, when the population of the Cape tripled in size, the hours could be long and grueling as deaths by misadventure increased ten-fold. It was thankless work and it could be depressing at times. But like every other endeavor she pursued, she had thrown herself into it freely and completely.

In the years after her divorce, she had taken little interest in romantic pursuits. She had been on a handful of dates, but most of those had been only to pacify her mother who kept telling her that she was leading a sad and lonely life. It was somewhat true, but she had come to embrace the emptiness as a kind of manifest destiny. Happiness was a modern construct. Generations of adults prior to the twentieth century had not expected to be happy or fulfilled. In the words of Henry David Thoreau, most had led "lives of quiet desperation." She wondered why her own life should be any different.

This morning, Abby felt the stirrings of an entirely different mindset. It occurred to her that, because of her dreary outlook, she had failed to notice the remarkable man who had been working alongside her for the past six years. There was a fascinating dichotomy to Thom. At times, he was reticent and inscrutable and she had seen him get the upper hand in more than one violent altercation. But he had also been a comforting presence to her on multiple occasions, always listening, often providing sensitive and insightful advice when appropriate. Her recent discovery of his hidden talents—cooking, gardening, and carpentry among others—set him apart from most of the men she had ever met. He was a genuine Renaissance man.

Or "a keeper" as her mother might have said.

It was just her luck that she'd have this epiphany at the worst of all possible times. She could tell that Thom was at least mildly interested in her. He seemed to perk up whenever she was around and, more than once, she had noticed him admiring her physical attributes when he didn't think she was paying attention. But how could she pursue a relationship with him in the midst of a bizarre and sordid murder investigation? To her, it didn't seem appropriate.

Abby sat up on the futon and glanced at the antique mission clock on the wall. It was 7:05. Thom had promised to drive her out to Pine Vista to pick up her car before he headed into the station. She and Thom had watched the news before turning in last night. The primary focus shifted to Dave Stancyck, the advertising executive who had discovered the body while walking his dog. It turned out that Stancyck was the one responsible for leaking initial information to WXTK—a local radio station. He had called his wife, who was the producer of the station's morning show. Stancyck seemed more than willing to be interviewed and had a number of gruesome details to offer. It was now common knowledge among anyone following the case that Randall had been decapitated. In light of this new revelation, Thom and Abby figured that the media blitz at Pine Vista had very likely subsided.

Thom's plan was to leave slightly before 8:00 so Abby was late and really needed to get herself in gear. She hustled to the bathroom to take a quick shower and get dressed. Her mind kept drifting back to the warmth and comfort of Thom's home. She thought about how wonderful it would be to live in such a peaceful setting.

***

Thom awoke with a childish thought—how he wished the army of reporters would stay put in Bourne so he could spend a little more time with Abby. He realized that this was neither rational nor professional, but the feeling gnawed at him nevertheless. While no one would ever fill the same space in his life that had been occupied by his wife Kayla and daughter Lily, he had come to realize over the past year or so that there was room for something more than the daily grind of his job and an occasional outing with his small circle of friends at the Laughing Gull Pub. As cliché as it sounded, he knew there was more room in his heart.

Abby was brilliant, funny and accomplished. With her lustrous auburn hair, expressive green eyes and shapely build, she had proved to be a regular distraction to him on the job. Thom had always been good at playing the role of the fixer. He was certain he could serve a useful purpose in Abby's life. He could show her how wonderful she was and that there could be happiness after pain. He felt it was a lesson they both could benefit from.

But how was he supposed to broach the topic with her considering their current circumstances? She had just lost her ex-husband and, though she had loathed the man, the excruciating memories of their time together had been reawakened. She was vulnerable and conflicted right now. Any advance he made on her could be construed as predatory. Given the vast amount of respect he had for Abby, it was the last thing he wanted. There was little choice but to wait and see if things developed naturally between them. As of the present, they clearly enjoyed each other's company and he thought that was a good start.

At 7:10 Thom headed into the shower, thinking about the potentially grueling day ahead. There was no telling where this murder investigation would lead. He was already exhausted from turning the same old facts over and over in his mind. He let the hot water rejuvenate his spirits. As he was toweling off, he had a wonderful idea. Before heading out to Bourne, he and Abby could stop by The Marshland and finish the breakfast that had been interrupted yesterday morning. It would give them a little more quality time together. He was pretty sure she'd be in no hurry to get back to her townhouse.

Before putting on his uniform shirt, Thom did something he hadn't done in quite some time. He grabbed the bottle of Ralph Lauren cologne that had been sitting on his dresser for ages and sprayed some on himself. He instantly felt silly and rushed to the bathroom to wash it off. That was when his cell phone rang. Stumbling back to the bedroom, he answered. It was Abby.

"Morning, Chief. You just about ready to hit the road?"

"Yeah, um … sure," he said, using an old t-shirt to wipe away the cologne. It was no use. Polo was a rather powerful scent. If he wanted to erase the evidence, he'd have to hop back in the shower.

"You okay, Chief?" Abby said after a brief pause.

"Great," he fumbled. "Couldn't be better. I'm just getting dressed."

Jesus, he thought. She's got me acting like a high school kid.

"Okay," she said in an odd voice, sensing the quirkiness of the exchange. "I was wondering if we could stop at The Marshland on the way out to Bourne. I've got a craving for one of their muffins."

"We can do that," he said, trying to regain his composure. "I didn't get any calls in the night, so apparently, there's nothing pressing at the station."

"Great."

"Yeah, so, I guess I'll meet you in the carport in a few minutes. I've still got to pull on some socks and shoes."

Smooth, Chief, he told himself. You really know how to lay on the charm.

She laughed pleasantly. "Well, good luck with that I guess. I'll see you in a few."

"Right, bye."

He snapped the phone shut, cursing himself for being so awkward.

2

By 8:05, they were in his Jeep on their way to The Marshland. Abby was filling the space between them with idle chatter. If she had noticed he was wearing cologne, she hadn't said anything. Thom liked how she started the day in an upbeat mood. That had not been his experience with women in general. Kayla and Lily had been somewhat taciturn in the morning. And his sister, Nancy, had been prone to tirades if she was asked to leave the bathroom so he could have a turn. He found this to be a refreshing change.

As he pulled onto Salt Marsh Lane, which would lead them to a series of side roads on their way to 6A, he noticed a black SUV traveling behind them at a considerable distance. He thought little of it until the vehicle was still with them as they approached the restaurant. He supposed this could be nothing out of the ordinary. The Marshland was among the most popular eateries in Sandwich and its location was ideal for commuters.

Thom swung into the parking lot and waited to see what the SUV would do. He was relieved when it continued past the restaurant and disappeared from view.

"What's wrong, Chief? You look like you've seen a ghost." Abby said.

"Nothing," he told her. "It looked like we had a tail there for a few minutes. I guess I was overreacting."

Again, Abby considered mentioning the man she had seen outside her townhouse yesterday morning but decided against it. "So are we eating here or taking our food on the road?" She asked.

"We're doing pretty good on time," he suggested. "Why don't we eat here?"

"Fine with me," she said agreeably.

They got out of the car and walked into the restaurant for the second consecutive morning. Business always seemed to come in waves at The Marshland and they had hit it just right. Aside from a few people sitting at the counter, they more or less had the place to themselves. The same waitress who had served them yesterday greeted them promptly and ushered them to a table facing the parking lot. As they sat down, Thom's stomach did a little flip. The black SUV had circled back around and was now idling outside in plain view. Thom noted that the driver was wearing over-sized sunglasses and a Boston Bruins tuk. Though the man's features were partially obscured, he appeared to be in his early sixties. As Abby settled into the booth, Thom apprised her of the situation.

"When you get a chance, take a look to my left at the black SUV in the parking lot. Try not to be obvious about it. I think the guy is watching us."

Abby followed Thom's instructions, maintaining a casual appearance. Sun was glaring off the windshield, but she could still make out the person behind the wheel. It was definitely the same man she had seen at Pine Vista. He was wearing a different hat, but there was no mistaking the face.

"Yup, I've seen him before," she said, picking up a menu. "He was outside my house yesterday morning. When I pulled up, he took off like a bat out of hell. The funny thing is, I was going to tell you about it and decided not to. I was worried you'd think I was being paranoid."

"Well, obviously you're not," Thom assured her. "The guy's been following us all the way from the marsh. I wonder who sent him."

"My first guess would be Randall's father," Abby said.

"Could be a reporter," Thom suggested.

"I don't think so. He was at my house long before the news trucks got there."

"With all the money Douglas Landry's got, you'd think he could afford to hire someone more professional. This guy's a clod. He's parked right outside the window. And don't even get me going on that ridiculous disguise."

Abby chuckled. "Still, he could be armed."

"You're right. One of the basic principles of police work is never to underestimate a situation. Could be he doesn't care we know he's there. That would make him a dangerous clod. And those are the worst kind."

"So what should we do?"

"Well, in about thirty seconds, I'm going to head into the kitchen and show them my badge. There's a door that leads to a dumpster on the backside of the parking lot. Hopefully, this guy won't see me coming from that direction."

"I assume you want me to stay put," Abby said.

"If you would," he replied politely. "If the waitress gets here before I'm finished, order me something tasty. I trust your judgment."

"All right. Be careful, Chief."

"I will."

Thom grabbed a menu, had a brief look then went through the motions of excusing himself from the table. The cook on duty was more than happy to grant him access to the back door. And as predicted, the guy in the SUV was oblivious to Thom's approach. He nearly jumped out of his seat when he noticed the Chief at his driver's side window holding a badge.

The guy rolled the window down and tried his best to act innocent. "You really gave me a start, officer. Is something wrong?"

"I don't know yet," said Burroughs in an authoritative tone. "Can I see some form of ID? And take off the sunglasses, would you?"

"Sure."

The man pulled off his shades and opened the glove compartment, producing a valid driver's license. His name was Philip Pullman. And he currently resided in suburban Boston.

"You're from Brookline I see. So what brings you to Sandwich, Mr. Pullman?"

"I heard the restaurants are good."

"They are, though I'm not sure why you followed us to this one. Are you lost or something?"

"I don't know what you're talking about."

"C'mon," Burroughs said impatiently. "I'd like to eat my breakfast while it's hot. Tell me what you're really doing here, or would you prefer we talk about it at the station? If we go that route, I should warn you that I'm a real bear when I'm hungry."

Pullman reached inside his jacket pocket and instantly found himself staring down the business end of Burroughs' Glock. His face registered alarm.

"Keep your hands where I can see them," the Chief barked.

"Okay, okay, let's not get jumpy. Jesus. I was just going to show you my badge."

"Badge?"

"Yeah, I'm a private investigator."

"All right," Burroughs said evenly. "I'm going to lower my weapon. Don't make any sudden movements. Take the badge out of your pocket nice and easy."

Pullman followed instructions as Burroughs returned the gun to his waistband holster. The badge was legitimate.

"So who hired you?" the Chief inquired.

"I'm not supposed to tell you that."

"Of course you aren't, but you don't have much of a choice at this point. There are at least three things I could cite you for. For starters, you need to get your vehicle inspected. It was due in September."

"All right, fine," Pullman conceded. "I didn't really want this job anyway. I was hired by Douglas Landry. He's a hotshot doctor from Boston."

"I know who he is. What exactly did he hire you to do?"

"He asked me to keep tabs on his former daughter-in-law. Said that she's been blackmailing his son."

"Did he give you any details?"

"Yeah, apparently it has something to do with some pornographic videos. The son has been paying big money to keep them off the internet. Just about bankrupted him I guess."

"So how long have you been following Doctor Rhodes?"

"Coupla days. She had a date with her ex-husband on the night he was killed. I followed them to a restaurant in Brewster. They seemed to be getting along just fine, which didn't make any sense to me if she was blackmailing him."

This is getting pretty interesting, thought Burroughs. "Tell me more about this date," he prodded.

"They went to a place called Chillingworth's—it's one of those upscale joints. I wasn't dressed for it, so I ended up sitting in my car. I had a pretty good view of their table from the parking lot. They had a couple of drinks and ordered some appetizers, but then I nodded off before the main course arrived."

"You're kidding me, right?" said the Chief, stifling the urge to laugh out loud.

"Hey, I'm sixty-five years old," Pullman countered defensively, "and it was getting late."

"Right. Sorry. Go on," Burroughs prompted him.

"There's not much more to tell. A motorcycle woke me up. It pulled into the parking lot. The rider got off and was futzing around with his saddlebags. It looked like he had a bunch of old rags in there and there was hay spilling out."

Burroughs' heart started hammering in his chest. "Did you get a look at the guy?" he asked.

"Yeah—he took his helmet off and glanced over at me. He had spiky black hair and light brown skin. He was tall and stocky and there was a scar along his jawline."

"How about the license plate?" Burroughs inquired hopefully.

"Nah. But I know what kind of bike it was—a Suzuki GSX. My son has a black one. This one was yellow."

"All right. So did you see Doctor Rhodes leave?"

"Yeah. She and Landry's son, the other doctor, took separate cars. They headed back toward Sandwich with the motorcycle on their tail. I tried to follow, but got stuck behind a slow-moving tractor-trailer and ended up losing them. I headed back to Pine Vista instead. I feel pretty crappy about the whole thing. If I had done my job right, things might have turned out differently."

"Don't beat yourself up over it," said Burroughs. "Who's to say you could have prevented the murder if you had been there?"

"I could have at least gotten a look at the killer."

"Well, the guy on the motorcycle is definitely a person of interest. If I put together a list of Suzuki GSX owners in the area, do you think you could come to the station and take a look at some driver's license photos?"

Pullman considered the request and shrugged. "Yeah, sure. I can do that."

"Do you have a card?"

"Of course."

Pullman reached into his pocket and produced a business card. Burroughs gave it a cursory glance then tucked it away.

"You said you didn't want this job. So why did you take it?"

"I was a Boston detective for over twenty years. I took a coupla bullets in the line of duty and opted for early retirement. Even with a full pension, I couldn't make ends meet. So I took up private investigating. I know I've gotten sloppy and I probably should've hung it up years ago. But Landry offered me twice my usual rate. I couldn't turn it down. I've got a son I'm trying to put through college."

"I see," said Burroughs. "Well, I hate to interfere with your livelihood, but Doctor Rhodes is in protective police custody and I'm going to have to ask you to back off. Tell your employer she isn't blackmailing anyone."

"Yeah, I kinda figured that," Pullman replied. "I did a background check. Everything came up clean. She seems straight as an arrow to me."

"She is," Burroughs affirmed.

"Hey, let me know when you put that list together. I'm happy to help you guys out."

"I appreciate it," said Burroughs, extending his hand.

Pullman shook it.

"I'll be in touch," Burroughs promised.

With that, he headed back into the restaurant to have breakfast with Abby. He didn't notice the vehicle following Pullman out of the parking lot.

3

It was a breakfast that was doomed to never happen. No sooner had their food arrived when Abby's cell phone rang. Thom salted his eggs and hash while she engaged in a brief conversation.

"Oh … I see … That's unfortunate. Were you able to ID the victim? Okay. I'm on my way."

She ended the call and stuffed the phone in the outside pocket of her fleece.

"Thom, I hate to do this to you, but I have to get to work right away. Can you take me home now?"

"Of course. What's going on?"

"Well, you're going to find this pretty hard to believe—"

"Try me."

"The guy you just talked to, Philip Pullman, was involved in a fatal crash in the Bourne rotary."

She was right. Thom could scarcely believe the news. And he was sorry to hear it. Not only had Pullman seemed like a halfway decent guy, but his death was a serious blow to the investigation.

***

When they got to Pine Vista, Abby and Thom were pleased to discover that the reporters had packed up and left. Off chasing juicier leads, they supposed.

Abby promised to call with details of Pullman's death as soon as she had them. Thom decided it was time to stop by the Landry offices in Plymouth and poke around a little. It would be helpful to know who Randall had met with on the day of the murder. And, if he ran into Douglas, maybe they could address their differences face to face.

Before making the twenty-mile trek, Thom phoned the station. Annie was on desk duty and her nasally voice filled his ear.

"Sandwich Police Department."

"Morning, Annie, it's Thom."

"Hey, Chief. How are ya?"

"Not bad. Anything interesting going on?"

"Nope. Everything's pretty quiet right now, but I did hear there was a major traffic accident out in Bourne."

"Yeah, I heard it, too. Listen, I'm following some leads in that Landry case and I have to take a run up to Plymouth. Is Barber in yet?"

"Not yet, Chief."

"Okay. Well, I've got an assignment for him. Tell him to make a list of every Suzuki GSX owner within fifty miles of the Landry murder site. Then tell him to narrow that list down to just the yellow ones. Got that? It's real important."

"Yeah, I got it, Chief."

"Okay, I'll see you in maybe an hour or so."

"Right. Good luck."

"Thanks, Annie."

With that, Burroughs headed toward the Sagamore Bridge Connector which would take him to the Mid Cape Highway on his way to Route 3.

Plymouth had been the site of the original Pilgrim landing in 1620. There were multiple points of interest there, including the Plimouth Plantation—a living museum complete with a seventeenth century English village and full-scale replica of the Mayflower ship. Burroughs had visited the plantation once when he first moved to the Cape but hadn't been back since. Like most year-rounders, he left the tourist attractions to the tourists.

The town itself was a scenic but bustling community situated on Cape Cod Bay. Spanning several exits along Route 3, it had become significantly commercialized over the past several decades. There were malls, fast food chains, and convenience stores ad nauseam. Douglas Landry's Plymouth office, which he had shared with his son until recently, was used for consults and follow-ups only. Actual procedures were performed locally at Jordan Hospital. Special cases were handled at the affiliated Beth Israel Deaconess Center in Boston. Beth Israel was among the best in the state, invariably appearing alongside Mass General and Brigham Women's whenever hospital rankings were issued.

The South Shore Cosmetic Surgery offices were located in a handsome brick and glass building overlooking the bay. It was the only modern structure on the block. Everything else dated back to the nineteenth century and looked like it belonged on a postcard. Burroughs pulled his car into a parking spot and checked his dashboard clock. It was a little after 9:00. Scattered vehicles in the lot indicated that the clinic was open for business. He exited his car and entered the building.

A revolving glass door opened on a lavishly adorned waiting room cluttered with Ottoman furniture, ficus plants, and expensive looking artwork. The receptionist served as yet another decorative item with her bleached blonde hair and sunless tan. By the size of her chest, it appeared as if she was not only an employee but a client as well. She smiled genially at Burroughs as he entered. The way she looked him up and down suggested that she was interested and available. He guessed that she was at least fifteen years his junior.

"Morning Officer, what can I do for you?"

"Morning, Danielle," He said, spying the nameplate on her desk. "I'm Chief Thom Burroughs from the Sandwich Police Department and I was wondering if I could ask you a few questions."

Her perma-smile instantly evaporated. She made a little noise of displeasure. "He said you might stop by."

"Who?"

"The doctor."

"Is he in?"

"No. He's on-call."

Burroughs nodded and smiled, trying to figure a way back into her good graces. "That's a terrific blouse you're wearing. Is that Prada?"

"Louis Vuitton," she corrected him.

"Nice. I love the patterns."

"I'm not supposed to talk to you," she said, her lips set in a pouty expression.

"The doctor told you that?"

She nodded. Burroughs was certain that she wasn't terribly bright.

"Well, unfortunately, your boss doesn't get to make those kinds of decisions. I'm a police officer and this is a murder investigation."

He may as well have just screamed the "f-word." She gazed feverishly around the waiting room with a panicked look on her face. Satisfied that there were no patients in proximity, she appeared to relax a little. She motioned with her index finger for him to come closer. He did. Her breath smelled like bubble gum.

"I could lose my job if I tell you anything," she said, her voice barely above a whisper.

"I promise you it won't come to that," he assured her. "You're bound by law to cooperate with this investigation. If you don't, it could be considered obstruction of justice."

Her eyes went wide. They were pretty eyes—a deep shade of blue. Burroughs could tell she was impressed with his authority.

"Okay," she said. "I do know something. But you gotta promise me I won't get fired."

Burroughs put his hand on his chest. "I solemnly swear," he said, astonished by his own corniness.

"Last week, a man came into the office and demanded to see Doctor Landry."

"Which doctor?" He asked.

"Randall. Douglas is hardly ever here, though I'm sure we'll be seeing a little more of him now, 'cuz, you know ..."

"Okay, got it," he said. "Go on."

"Well, this man was pretty scary looking. He had shifty eyes and scars on his face. He wouldn't tell me who he was or what it was about. He didn't have an appointment either. But Doctor Landry agreed to see him anyway. They went into the doctor's office and a huge argument broke out. They were shouting at each other. Nothing like that has ever happened in all the time I've worked here. Nurse Rachael and I got so shook up, we were going to call the cops."

"Were there other patients around?"

"No. It was five o'clock. We were getting ready to close up for the night."

"What was the argument about?"

"Well, the rooms are pretty soundproof, but they were being awful loud. I definitely heard them yelling about money. Aside from that, I couldn't tell you much."

"Interesting," Burroughs mused. "And you'd never seen this guy around here before."

"Nope. Even if I did, I wouldn't be able to tell you. We have these things called HIPPA regulations. They protect the rights of patients."

"Yup, I know what they are, Danielle. Did you know that a murder investigation supersedes HIPPA? Of course, you have the option not to talk to us, but we can subpoena your records. And again, your lack of cooperation could be construed as an obstruction."

Poor Danielle appeared flustered by all the big words. "Nurse Rachael thought the guy looked familiar. She didn't know his name, but she figured maybe Douglas or Randall had worked on him at some point."

"Is Nurse Rachael in today?"

"Nope. She's out on maternity leave. She got done last Friday."

Burroughs didn't see any pressing need to speak with the nurse anyway. He was getting plenty of information out of Danielle.

"So what did this guy look like?"

"Well, like I said, he had scars. They were along his jaw line. It looked like he'd had some serious work done. He was tall and pretty well built like he lifted weights. And he had spiky black hair with light-brown skin. I don't think it was a tan. He could have been a Pakistani or something."

The description was identical to the one Pullman had provided for the man on the motorcycle. This could be a real breakthrough except that Pullman wasn't around to identify the cyclist anymore.

"Did you see the man drive off?"

"No. Doctor Landry came out of his office in the middle of the argument and told us to go home. We were both kinda spooked and it was just about time to leave so we didn't stick around."

"On your way out, did you happen to notice a motorcycle in the parking lot?"

Please say yes, Burroughs thought.

The receptionist flipped her hair unconsciously before answering. It was a move any number of men her age would have found attractive. "No. Sorry. There could have been one I suppose, but I really wasn't paying attention."

Dammit, Burroughs' inner voice cursed.

"If I were to come back here with some pictures, do you think you could identify the man?"

"Definitely. I never forget a face."

"Okay. You're being very helpful, Danielle, and I appreciate it. There's just one more thing then I'll be on my way. I'm wondering who the doctors met with over the last few days. You guys must have an appointment book around."

She bit her fingernails uncertainly. He noticed that the nails were chewed down to the quick. Everything else about her was immaculately groomed. "I'm not supposed to give out information like that. I could lose my job."

"It would be strictly confidential. And it would help us solve your boss's murder. I'm sure you want the killer brought to justice, don't you?" Again, he was surprised at how trite he could be when a situation demanded it.

"Absolutely," she answered with conviction.

She grabbed the appointment book, which had been sitting in front of her the entire time, and carried it with her to a Xerox machine located in the rear of the reception area. She hastily copied a few pages and handed them to Burroughs, glancing nervously up the hallway to her right before she did. "I better not get fired over this," she fretted. "I can barely afford my apartment in Duxbury as it is."

"Don't worry, Danielle," Burroughs said in a comforting tone. "You can't be fired for cooperating with law enforcement officials. You've done the Sandwich Police Department a great service today. Thanks so much."

It was definitely time for him to make an exit. Everything he had told Danielle about obstruction of justice and subpoenaing records was true. But Douglas Landry reserved the right to hang onto those records until formally compelled to release them. This visit had proved far more fruitful than Burroughs had anticipated and there was no sense hanging around until someone better informed and far less friendly interfered.

"I may be back with some photos for you to look at," he told Danielle, turning to leave.

"I hope you find the killer," she said. "Randall Landry was one of the sweetest men I've ever worked for."

Looking the way she did, Burroughs was not surprised by that statement one bit.

"Goodbye, Danielle. Thanks again."

And with that, he exited through the revolving glass door.

***

What a mess, Abby thought as she surveyed the accident scene. The Bourne Rotary was one of the most congested intersections in the region. Designed to direct traffic toward the seven-mile waterway separating the peninsula from mainland Massachusetts, the rotary actually created a dangerous bottleneck situation at rush hour. Abby had responded to numerous crashes here in the past.

Pullman's car had veered into the grass infield in the center of the rotary and come to rest near the shrubbery that spelled out the words "Cape Cod." Troopers had set up road flares and were signaling traffic around the tangle of rescue vehicles that had converged upon the scene.

After locating the Officer in Charge and receiving clearance to investigate the wreck, Abby crossed the grassy area to Pullman's vehicle. According to witnesses, it had careened across two lanes of traffic, collided with another car then spun off the road. The tailgate had sustained heavy damage and one of the passenger side windows was shattered, but it didn't appear to be a fatal crash upon initial inspection. The cause of Pullman's death became abundantly clear to Abby after she viewed the body, which was slumped across the front seat. The implications were staggering.

He had been shot in the head.

For the second time in a span of two hours, Burroughs could scarcely believe his ears. He had been pulling onto the ramp from Samoset Street to Route 3 when he received Abby's phone call via his Bluetooth device. Upon hearing the news about Pullman, he nearly collided with a guardrail.

"Shot?" Thom said incredulously, correcting the Jeep's trajectory. "This is heading off the rails fast."

"No kidding," Abby agreed. "I'd be lying if I told you it didn't make me a little nervous. We're talking about the guy who was hired to follow me. Kinda makes you wonder who's next."

"I seriously doubt you have anything to worry about," he assured her. "The killer could easily have taken you out along with Randall at the overlook."

"Yeah, I've thought about that. Do you think Pullman was killed by the same guy?"

"I don't know if it was the same guy, but the two events are obviously connected."

Thom could hear a symphony of noise in the background. "Sounds pretty chaotic there," he commented.

"Yeah. They're taking the body to my headquarters in Bourne so I can run some tests. I'll probably have to call in a ballistics expert. I'm going to be busy for a while, but we should definitely touch base soon."

"You're welcome out at my place for dinner again," he offered.

"That'd be wonderful," she said. "But I really don't want you to go to any trouble this time."

"Would you be happier if we picked up some Chinese takeout?"

"I love Chinese," she affirmed.

"Okay, I'll wait for you. Give me a call when you get free."

"I will. Thanks." There was a pause before she added, "Be careful, Thom. I know you're a tough guy and all, but Pullman was killed right after he talked to you. Don't forget that."

"Yeah," he told her. "It's going to be difficult to put it out of my mind, actually."

"I know. Well, gotta run. I'll call you."

"Great. Bye, Abby."

"Bye, Chief."

He pressed a button on the dashboard and ended the conversation. As much as he dreaded it, these latest developments necessitated a call to Lieutenant Carlson. With a twenty-five minute drive ahead of him, he figured there was no time like the present. Pulling Carlson's card out of his wallet, he dialed the number using the Bluetooth's voice command feature. The lieutenant actually sounded somewhat pleased to hear from him.

"Hey, Chief, what's new?"

"Quite a bit, actually."

Burroughs relayed nearly every relevant piece of information he had received in the past sixteen hours or so, including the bit about Randall's pornographic videos. He excluded details of his trip to Plymouth since that was technically out of his jurisdiction. Carlson was surprised to hear about Burroughs' encounter with Pullman and the shocking twist that followed.

"Man, this is turning into a bad detective novel," the lieutenant remarked. "So Doctor Rhodes got called to the scene?"

"Yeah, I just talked to her. She said she was going to get a ballistics consult."

"I'd like to see the results. On a different note, you'll be interested to hear that my guys talked to a few of the folks who attended that costume party in Harwich Wednesday night. Turns out there *was* a scarecrow there after all. According to one of the event's organizers, people were asked to show up in costume and keep their identities secret until awards for the best costumes were given out. Guests were required to show a generic invitation at the door, but aside from that, there was no formal check-in. Over a hundred people showed up."

"So nobody knows who the scarecrow was," Burroughs presumed.

"Right. But he did speak to at least one guest—a Doctor LaMoyne. The guy's a highly regarded dermatologist and he regularly assisted with Randall's procedures at Beth Israel Hospital. Apparently, the man in the scarecrow costume asked LaMoyne where he could find Randall. According to LaMoyne, Randall had been bragging about getting back together with his ex-wife for months and had skipped out on the fundraiser at the last minute so he could wine and dine her at Chillingworth's."

"So Randall's name was on the guest list?"

"Yup. The lady in charge of invitations confirmed that he RSVP'd."

"Then our scarecrow must have known in advance that Randall was invited."

"It would appear so," Carlson agreed. "When LaMoyne told the scarecrow that Randall was at Chillingworth's, he left the party in a hurry."

"Did LaMoyne recognize anything about the guy?"

"Nope. But the description he gave me of the costume more or less matched the one you got from that lady out at the farm. What's it called again?"

"The Crow Farm."

"Right," said Carlson, sounding uncharacteristically animated. "So the pieces of the puzzle are starting to fit. I think it's fair to presume that the guy in the costume and the guy on the motorcycle are one and the same. If that's the case, then we can place him at multiple locations in a credible time frame all in connection to Randall's murder."

"I wonder if the guy had an invitation to the party or if he crashed it," Burroughs mused.

"Well, anyone who would steal a costume from a farm stand strikes me as a party crasher," Carlson replied.

"So how did he know that Randall was invited? And how did he know to approach LaMoyne? He must have recognized him."

"That's a reasonable assumption," said Carlson. "I'll have my guys talk to LaMoyne again. While they're at it, they can interview every guest along with all the organizers and members of the banquet staff. That ought to burn some man hours. It's a pretty long list."

"Speaking of lists," Burroughs confessed, "I stopped by Landry's office in Plymouth and talked the receptionist into photocopying the appointment schedules of both doctors."

There was a pregnant pause.

"You do realize I've got half a dozen guys working this case, right Chief?"

"I do," Burroughs said defensively. "But I was feeling motivated by Pullman's death."

"You're ambitious," Carlson acknowledged. "I'll give you that. Landry's office was on our roll of places worth checking out, but I guess I can cross it off the registry. If you promise to share any leads, I'll turn my back on the fact that Plymouth is out of your jurisdiction by a long shot."

"Fair enough," Burroughs conceded, feeling the first spark of partiality toward Carlson. The man had sparse social skills, but he was fairly reasonable when it came to protocol. "I'm headed back to the station now. I've got my detective working on a list of Suzuki GSX owners in the Bay area. I'll take a look at Landry's appointment schedule when I get to Sandwich."

"Sounds good," said Carlson. "We'll be in touch."

There was a click as he ended the call. It was as close as he had ever come to saying goodbye. It wasn't much, but it was a start, Burroughs supposed.

5

Hours later, when Abby was sitting at his breakfast bar enjoying a cup of tea, Thom pitched a working theory of Randall's murder to her.

"Here's how I think it played out," he began. "The blackmailer showed up at Randall's office and there was a major blowout. When Randall told him his finances had gone dry, the blackmailer made plans to kill the doctor at the fundraiser in Harwich. He stole a disguise he had seen at a local farm stand, knowing it wouldn't be traceable to any costume shop, and crashed the party holding the murder weapon in plain view … talk about nerve. But Randall wasn't there. He was at Chillingworth's in Brewster trying to sweet talk his ex-wife, who took half of his assets a few years ago, into rekindling their relationship."

"For the record, I put most of those assets to good use," Abby interjected.

"That fact has never been in dispute," Thom replied, validating her statement. "At any rate, the guy took off his costume, hopped on his motorcycle and made the short jump up to Brewster. He ended up being spotted by Philip Pullman in the Chillingworth's parking lot. He followed you guys out to the overlook, keeping a safe distance so he wouldn't be noticed. Now I know you've heard this question before, but try to think, did you see a yellow motorcycle pull up at any point while you were at the site?"

She closed her eyes and tried to picture the murder scene, but ended up drawing a blank. "Honestly, I didn't. On the observation deck, it was hard to hear over the wind and the waves. And Randall kept putting his hands on me, so I was pretty distracted."

"I assume you had your backs to the marsh."

"Yeah, we were facing the bay … most of the time anyway."

"So the cyclist could easily have cut the engine, killed the lights and walked his bike down a stretch of the access road without either of you noticing. The marsh grass would have hidden him while he changed into his scarecrow outfit."

"Yeah, I guess so," Abby replied. "Our argument got heated at one point and we were both pretty oblivious."

"We keep coming back to the same question," said Thom. "What's the significance of the costume? It had already served its purpose, so why put it on again?"

"I don't know," Abby said, puzzled. "To hide his identity, maybe."

There was a lull in the conversation as they both considered the possibilities.

"Did you get a chance to look at Douglas's appointment book?" Abby inquired.

"I started to, but I kept getting pulled in a million different directions. Detective Barber is still checking out that list of motorcycle owners. He told me he should have it narrowed down by Monday. Did your examination of Pullman's body turn up anything interesting?"

"He died of a single gunshot wound to the head—fired at moderately close range. He would have survived the accident otherwise. I called in our ballistics expert who works out of Brewster. The bullet was a .45 caliber hollow point fired from a Ruger P97. Based on the entry wound, Pullman was shot from behind. The movies make it look easy, but to hit somebody in a moving vehicle from another moving vehicle is quite a feat. To do it with a single shot is nothing short of miraculous. So the shooter was either very skilled or very lucky. There was a quite a bit of traffic in the rotary, but only two drivers—the ones directly involved in the accident—were detained for questioning. The rest continued on their merry way. Neither of the drivers who ended up being interviewed had any helpful information."

"The DOT must have cameras stationed at that rotary. It's one of the busiest interchanges in the area."

"They do," Abby confirmed. "Three in fact—northbound, southbound and at the foot of the mainland side of the bridge. But the one with a continuous live feed is out of order. The other two provide time elapsed stills at fifteen-second intervals."

"Might be worth checking out," said Thom.

"Yeah, I'm sure somebody will. But my job is more or less finished at this point. The family signed a release to have the body transferred to a funeral home in Quincy."

"That's too bad," Thom commented pensively. "He told me he had a son he was putting through college."

"He had a daughter, too," Abby informed him. "They both came to identify the body."

Abby sighed heavily and sipped her tea. The atmosphere in the room had taken a decidedly gloomy turn.

"So, what's next?" Thom said.

"You mean with the investigation?"

"No, I mean dinner."

"Oh," she said, taken off guard by the abrupt segueway. "You had mentioned Chinese takeout earlier."

"I've got a better idea," he said. "I think it would do us both some good to get out for a little while. There's a great Irish pub in Dennis that's run by some friends of mine."

"The Laughing Gull," she said.

"You know it?"

"Of course. I haven't been there in ages."

"So what do you think?"

"I think it's a great idea."

"All right. I'll take you there under one condition."

"What's that?"

"No more shop talk for now. I promise not to mention anything even remotely related to the case for the next couple of hours or so."

"Agreed," Abby said brightly.

6

Upon entering the pub, they were greeted by the bearded giant standing behind the bar. Abby figured he must be at least six and a half feet tall. He looked at Thom and rolled his eyes.

"I told you last time I'd put the dogs on you if you came in here again," his voice boomed. Then he winked at Abby and added with a broad grin, "Of course you can stay, ma'am."

Thom laughed heartily as the man came out from behind the bar and gave him a bear hug.

"Missed you, buddy," Thom said. "Sorry it's been so long."

The man extended his hand to Abby. "Paul McLeod, owner and proprietor of this humble establishment. Welcome."

Abby's hand completely disappeared inside Paul's as she introduced herself.

"You never told me about this lovely little lass," Paul said to Thom. "You might as well break it off now. She's way too good for you."

"Mind your manners, Paul," scolded a dark-haired woman in a green collared shirt. She was carrying a tray of drinks hurriedly toward the dining area which was separated from the bar by a wainscoted half wall. She smiled warmly at Thom. "I'll be over to say hello in a minute," she told him.

"That's my own lovely little lass," Paul said to Abby. "She's rather fond of bossing me around."

"Well, somebody's got to keep you in line," Thom joked, evoking a clamorous round of laughter from his friend.

"Do you folks want to sit at the bar or at one of the tables?" Paul inquired courteously.

Abby and Thom both scanned the dining area. Being 7:35 on a Friday, the restaurant was predictably packed. The bar was far less crowded at the moment.

"I don't mind sitting at the bar," Abby said.

"Okay," Thom agreed. "But I should warn you in advance that Paul will probably flirt with you all evening."

Abby smiled. "I think I can handle that," she said.

"You see?" said Paul with mock arrogance. "Women can't resist my Celtic charms."

Paul returned to his spot behind the bar as Abby and Thom grabbed a pair of available stools. A large flat screen television was tuned to a Boston Bruins game. Most of the patrons at the bar were completely engrossed. It was early in the first period and the B's were losing to the New York Rangers by a score of 1-0.

"I love hockey," Abby said.

"Really," Thom replied, sufficiently impressed. "What's your team?"

"The Bruins of course. My Dad used to take me to the old Boston Garden when I was younger. We even saw a Stanley Cup game in '88. The Bruins lost to Edmonton, 6-3. Wayne Gretzky had 4 assists."

Paul set a pair of menus in front of them and joined the conversation. "At least you got to see a whole game. I happened to be in attendance at the ill-fated Game 4," he said.

"Yikes. I feel bad for you," Abby consoled him. "First the fog and then the power failure at the Garden. The hockey gods were really conspiring against the Bruins that night but at least it's a game that everyone remembers."

Paul fixed Thom with a sober look. "The woman knows her hockey. If you blow it with her, I may have to permanently banish you from this restaurant."

Thom was about to explain that he and Abby were just friends when Paul's wife Karee arrived on the scene. She wrapped her arms around Thom's neck and planted a wet kiss on his cheek.

"It's good to see you, stranger. We were wondering when you were going to stop in."

"Where's Molly tonight?"

Thom was referring to Paul and Karee's daughter who was currently in the process of finishing up her master's degree.

"She's back at MIT for one more semester," Karee informed Thom. "She hasn't been making it home on the weekends lately. I think the schoolwork is really starting to pile up. I'll tell her you said hello. Hey, who's your date?"

Thom proceeded with a formal introduction. The two women shook hands affably.

"Any friend of Thom's is a friend of ours," Karee said sincerely. "So what can we get you to drink, Abby?"

"It'd be a shame not to sample the house brew," Abby remarked.

Paul smiled appreciatively. 'I think I'm in love," he said to Thom.

Karee swatted Paul playfully with her bar towel. "Did Thom warn you that my husband is an incorrigible flirt?" She asked Abby.

"He did, actually," Abby told her, grinning from ear to ear.

"Get to work," Karee scolded Paul. "I've got to check on a couple of food orders, but I'll be back. I'm watching you, husband."

And with that, she hustled into the kitchen.

Though the night was still young, Abby couldn't remember the last time she'd had this much fun.

7

The cargo van was rocked by the passage of a tractor trailer bearing a Stop & Shop logo. In the driver's seat, the man with the scars was displeased with himself. He had acted somewhat impulsively. Now there were two dead bodies attracting unwanted attention. The beheading had been mildly satisfying at least—a ritual punishment that had survived for centuries among men of his faith and calling. But he'd have to be careful from here on out to make any necessary deaths appear natural.

After disposing of Randall Landry, he had spent a sleepless night wondering if it wouldn't have been wiser to kill Doctor Rhodes as well, but she seemed like a rather charitable woman. And he had been in full costume when their paths had crossed at the overlook—unlike that bungling fool Pullman who had spotted him in Brewster. He wondered what Pullman had said to the officer in The Marshland parking lot. He would hate to have to get rid of a cop, too. That would really bring the heat down on him.

The man with the scars allowed the commuters along Route 6 to speed past him. Some of them beeped their horns as they did, but he wasn't about to risk breaking the speed limit. After watching the evening news during his dinner break at the health care center in Hyannis, he had made an important decision. He had used the nurses' key to gain access to the pharmaceutical closet. He was careful to straighten the shelves so they appeared undisturbed. It would be a few days before anyone noticed the missing needle-free injector and the two intravenous drugs he had helped himself to. He had put in his resignation two weeks ago and tonight was his last shift. By the time the stolen items were discovered, he'd be off the grid.

He had acquired the van, an aging Chevy Express, from a tract of vacant summer homes in Yarmouth. After hot-wiring the engine, he had returned the stolen motorcycle—a spiffy little Suzuki GSX model—to the neighboring garage he'd taken it from a few days earlier. Starting the bike without a key had been easy. All he had to do was bridge the coils with a piece of electrical wire. He made sure to wipe the bike clean of prints before driving off in the borrowed van.

Now he was on his way to take care of some unpleasant business in Weston, which was located roughly seventeen miles from Boston. One particular resident of the affluent suburb needed to be dealt with posthaste. The man with the scars reached across the passenger side and opened the glove compartment. Pushing a Ruger P97 pistol out of the way, he grabbed a Ziploc bag of dried apricots and popped one into his mouth.

8

On the ride home from Dennis, Abby must have thanked Thom half a dozen times for the evening out. She had found McLeod's Ale much to her liking and had consumed enough of it to make her just a little tipsy. Thom had indulged in one beer during their dinner then switched to soda. They had stayed for the entire hockey game, which the Bruins won in dramatic fashion. Paul and Abby had engaged in a lively debate about the futility of shootouts, which pitted goalies against offensive players in one-on-one scenarios. Back in the day, games were declared ties if neither team scored during a standard overtime period. Abby and Paul, who were both purists, preferred the way things used to be. A longstanding tradition at the *Laughing Gull Pub*, every patron was entitled to a free glass of house ale each time the Bruins won. Paul had given out quite a few tonight after Boston came out on top, 4-3.

Abby and Thom both agreed that she should spend another night at his guest cottage. Though she wasn't openly intoxicated, her blood level was likely over the legal limit. That's the last thing Abby needed at this point—to end up with a DUI. She had been concerned about not having the necessary toiletries on hand, but Thom assured her he kept the cottage well stocked with all the pertinent supplies. She found this a little unusual for a man who rarely hosted company. But then, nothing about Thom was particularly ordinary.

Thom was pleased with the way the evening had turned out. Abby had hit it off in spectacular fashion with both Paul and Karee, prompting an invitation to the winter party they hosted at their home every year. Paul usually showed up alone, but it would be nice having someone accompany him for a change. In particular, it would be nice spending another evening with Abby. He was a little sorry that this night was coming to an end and he felt compelled to explain something to her before it did.

"Just so you know," he said awkwardly, "I never told my friends that you and I were in a relationship. They both just assumed that we were. I tried to tell Paul a couple of times, but he never let me finish."

Of course, Abby had been aware of the situation, but it hadn't caused her any concern. The McLeod's were charming people and the idea of being in a relationship with Thom was far from objectionable.

"It's all right," Abby said. "I've been accused of far worse things in the past forty-eight hours. I can handle suspicions of being your girlfriend."

Girlfriend.

The word sounded so odd to her after she said it but not the least bit unpleasant.

Thom was thinking precisely the same thing.

9

Located in the Metro-West Boston suburbs, Weston was the wealthiest community in Massachusetts with a median household income of over $150,000. This was quite apparent to the man with the scars as he cruised slowly down Wellesley Street which was lined with extravagant old houses. Using the directions he had gotten from the MapQuest website, he found his way to Douglas Landry's home, which was an expansive Victorian estate. The house was narrow and tall with a multitude of towers and turrets. Large bay windows were stationed on all sides, many of them composed of handsome stained glass. Like Landry's personality, the man with the scars found the home revoltingly pretentious. He pulled up to the curb and, posing as a colleague from Beth Israel Medical Center, placed a call to the doctors' exchange. The operator assured him that his call would be returned shortly. Landry waited roughly five minutes to dial the number he had provided.

"Doctor Wright, it's Doctor Landry returning your call."

"Don't hang up," the man with the scars said, disguising his voice. "I have information regarding the death of your son. I know who killed him, but it's too dangerous for me to go to the police."

There was a considerable pause.

"Doctor Landry, are you there?"

"Yes … go on," Landry said finally.

"I need money to get away. If the people involved find me, they'll kill me."

"Who is this?"

"Don't worry about who I am. Do you want to know who murdered your son?"

"Very much so," Landry snorted, his voice full of contempt.

"I've written directions to a diner where we can meet. It's in Waltham. I included my monetary demands as well. You'll find the information in your mailbox. Please check it and get back to me soon. If I don't hear from you in ten minutes, I'll assume you're not interested. There won't be a second chance."

The man with the scars had already exited the van and was crouched behind a hedgerow near Landry's front porch. He pulled the essential item from the pocket of his jacket and positioned himself to strike.

"Does this have anything to do with the videos?" Landry wondered.

"Not at all. My time's running short, Doctor. You have ten minutes starting now."

The man with the scars terminated the call. He was almost certain that Landry had completely bought his ruse. That assumption proved correct when Landry appeared on the front porch less than a minute later.

The doctor froze in stark terror as a figure emerged from the shadows. "Hey, I know you," he said incredulously as the man with the scars rushed toward him.

Those were his last words.

The man with the scars held the needle-free injector to Landry's neck and depressed the plunger. There was a loud click and a faint whoosh of air as he did so. Landry, clutching his chest, slumped to the porch almost immediately. The lethal injection he received was composed of Pavulon and potassium chloride, the same elixir used to execute death row inmates. Since the man with the scars didn't have the luxury of time, he opted not to stick around for the full minute it would take for Landry to die. His work nearly finished for the night, he hopped in the van and headed back toward Yarmouth.

10

Thom's first thought when his cell phone rang at 8:30 a.m. was that he was late for work. But as his head began to clear, he realized it was a Saturday. Though he was always on-call, a hazard of being a police chief, he was rarely pressed into duty on weekends during the offseason. Summer was a different story of course. The town of Sandwich hosted many popular events from July through August and he routinely found himself working six or seven days per week. Like most year-rounders, he preferred the relative tranquility of fall and spring.

As he fumbled for his phone on the nightstand, he was relieved to discover that it was Abby calling him from the guest house.

"Morning, Sunshine," she said cheerfully.

"How's it going?"

"I'm bored. Can I come over and play?"

"I'm not showered yet," he told her.

"Neither am I. I was thinking we could sit in our pajamas and catch up on the news."

"Yeah, I've been meaning to put a television out there. Do you actually wear pajamas?" He wondered.

"Ever since I was a little girl. It's a security thing."

"Me, too," he chuckled. "Not for security, just for … well, never mind. So do you prefer coffee or tea?"

"Surprise me," she said. "I'll be over in a couple of minutes."

"Okay," he said. "Bye."

Thom hopped out of bed and padded to the bathroom to brush his teeth. It was one thing to be lazing around the house with his hair uncombed and his pajamas on, but he had to maintain certain standards if he expected to entertain company of the female variety. He was just putting a pot of coffee on when he heard a knock at the carport door.

"It's open," he shouted across the kitchen.

Abby entered, looking immeasurably cute in flannel "Hello Kitty" pajamas. Her hair was swept up in a haphazard bun. She looked at his plain fleece lounge pants and remarked, "We've got to get you dressing with a little more flair."

"What would you prefer," he joked, "maybe Star Wars or Marvel superheroes?"

"Works for me," she giggled. "Hey, do you think it's a good idea to leave your door unlocked?"

"I'm a light sleeper and keep a loaded Glock next to my bed. It's intruders who should be worried."

"I guess so," she said.

"TV's in the living room," he told her, "if you can figure out how to turn it on. I can never seem to get the remotes in sync with each other."

"I've got the same problem at my house," she replied.

The kitchen was separated from the living room by a set of shuttered saloon style doors. Like every other room in the house, it was attractively decorated with mission style furniture and intriguing bric-a-brac. The flooring was of the wide plank variety found in old farmhouses with braided rugs stationed in the various sitting areas. One such area featured a wide row of mullioned windows that provided a fabulous view of the marsh.

Abby briefly paused to admire the scenery and then surveyed the three remotes lying on the television stand. She quickly determined that one of them corresponded to a DVD player and was therefore not a useful option. Of the remaining two, one commanded the satellite link and the other controlled the television itself. She managed to get the TV on in short order, tuning it to CNN, which had been carrying endless coverage of the Landry murder.

She expected to get a recap of stale facts but was surprised to find that there was actually some breaking news. A correspondent was stationed in front of Douglas Landry's mansion in Weston doing a live feed. A headline on the bottom of the screen proclaimed: "Douglas Landry Found Dead of a Heart Attack. Connection to His Son's Murder Has Not Been Established." Abby inadvertently dropped the remote, scooped it up then called toward the kitchen.

"Thom, you're going to want to come see this!"

Thom entered the living room a few seconds later carrying two cups of coffee that smelled strongly of vanilla. He offered one to Abby, but she didn't respond.

"What's going o …?"

His voice trailed off when he saw the television. The CNN Correspondent offered scant details of the incident. The body had been found lying on the front porch by a jogger. Time of death had not yet been determined. All evidence currently pointed to natural causes.

Yeah, right, thought Thom. Two Landry's in a seventy-two hour period. That's no coincidence. Though this was nothing short of an earth-shattering development, he was more concerned about how Abby might be feeling at the moment. He set the two coffees aside and put his arm comfortingly around her shoulder.

"I know this must be pretty rough," he said. "First your 'ex' and now your former father-in-law. It's a lot to take in."

"I'm okay," Abby assured him. "I mean, yeah … it's a little weird of course, but we were never close."

Thom could tell that something was troubling her. "So what's on your mind?" he wondered.

"Douglas Landry was a picture of health. He bragged about it all the time for as long as I knew him. Even Randall went on and on about it during our dinner Wednesday night. He chalked it up to superior Landry genes."

Thom became acutely aware that he was still touching Abby and pulled his arm away.

"This doesn't add up, Thom."

"I know," he said. "I'll get in touch with Carlson. I'm sure he knows more than the guys from CNN. By the way, your coffee's on the side table next to the couch."

Thom left her standing in the living room surfing channels for additional details. He headed back to his bedroom and grabbed his phone. Carlson's number was not yet programmed into his list of contacts. He made a note to get it done as he placed the call. After several rings, a robotic voice informed him dispassionately, "Your call has been transferred to an automated voice messaging system."

Thom ended the call, opting not to leave a message. He supposed even lieutenants took breaks from their cell phones once in a while. Instinctively, he dialed the station to see if anything was going on there. Duane Ward, the weekend dispatcher, answered. Thom didn't know Duane very well, but through their scattered interactions, found him to be both affable and competent.

"Morning, Duane, it's Chief Burroughs."

"Hey, Chief, how's it going?"

"Good thanks. Hey, has anyone called the station looking for me?"

"Nope. Nothing much going on around here right now. Murphy's out on a traffic stop, but that's about it."

"Okay, good. Let me know if anything big comes up."

"You got it. Have a nice weekend."

"Thanks. You, too. Bye, Duane."

Flustered, Thom sat down on the bed and expelled a heavy sigh. Though he hated to admit it, there really wasn't much of anything he could do at the moment. It was a helpless feeling.

11

In a quarry on the outskirts of New Martinsville, West Virginia, a man armed with a semi-automatic pistol stood guard by the chain that blocked the secluded access road. Inside the quarry, several of his associates were busy loading heavy crates of explosives into delivery trucks. One of them had disposed of the security guard on duty, who had been napping upon their arrival, and gained access to the supervisor's repository. It contained a treasure trove of valuable supplies—most notably a cache of wireless remote detonators.

It took two men to carry the dead guard to the loading area and deposit his body into one of the rented trucks. There were two of them on-site with enough combined cargo space to carry most of the explosive material the Appalachia Mining Company had on hand. That would be more than enough to stage the event.

The wind had picked up and the conspirators were forced to shield their eyes from the grit that was blowing across the quarry. Though the material they were loading was volatile and dangerous, there was not a man among them who would hesitate to die for the cause. They worked quickly and without fear.

When the trucks were loaded, the man guarding the access road was notified via a handheld transceiver. He removed the chain to allow the trucks a route of egress and placed a call to his contact in Massachusetts. As was customary, he didn't offer his name. He delivered a scripted message in his native language.

"Stage one complete. Rendezvous at selected location in roughly thirty-six hours."

***

Outside of Stockbridge, a garage door opened at a supply depot located along the Massachusetts Turnpike. A man in latex gloves entered the storage area and proceeded directly to a wall rack where hardhats and fluorescent safety vests were hanging in an asymmetrical row. He filled his arms with the materials and tossed them in the back of his Chevy SUV which bore the symbol of the Massachusetts Department of Transportation. Purchased from a local promotional company, the magnetic logo was a convincing facsimile of the ones belonging to actual DOT vehicles.

The man helped himself to several stacks of orange cones and placed them in the van with the rest of the pilfered items. His job nearly complete, he entered a five-digit code into the electronic keypad beside the door, chuckling to himself about how lax the security measures were around here.

Hopping into the driver's seat, the man removed his gloves and pulled back onto the Berkshire section of the Turnpike. Shortly into the ride, he took out his phone and dialed a number provided to him by one of his New York affiliates.

"I've got the materials," he said in Arabic.

He hung up.

The man with the scars felt nervous. Not the kind of nervousness accompanied by dread, but the kind that precedes a highly anticipated and welcome occurrence. After years of careful planning, the early stages of the event were finally underway.

Allahu Akbar!

He sat on the ground beside the borrowed van eating dried apricots and wondering what was taking his associates so long. They should have picked him up hours ago. Highly irritated, he pulled the burner phone out of his vest pocket and dialed their number again. It rang several times before someone finally answered.

"Hello."

"What's the holdup? I'm still waiting here in Yarmouth. It's a wonder I haven't been picked up by the police."

"I am sorry, Mullah. There have been some unavoidable delays. Seyed is on his way as we speak."

"Did you hear from the others?"

"Yes, and I received good news. The materials have been acquired."

"*Subhan'Allah!* Excellent, Aaban. I'm switching phones now. Don't try to call me on this one again."

The man with the scars snapped the prepaid phone shut and switched it off. He would dispose of it in a different location. Aaban's report pleased him greatly. At last, he was taking his final steps along the path to water. He looked up toward the morning sun and closed his eyes, envisioning a glorious afterlife.

Countdown

1

The rest of the weekend passed without any breaks in the Landry case. Though Douglas's death had been attributed to a heart attack, Abby and Thom were skeptical. They decided it might be prudent for Abby to stay in Sandwich awhile longer.

On Saturday afternoon they drove out to Bourne so Abby could grab some clothes. On the way back, they picked up some fresh haddock from Salty Lou's—a retail outlet located on Route 6A in East Sandwich. Thom knew the owners fairly well and had been buying most of his seafood from them for ages.

For dinner, he prepared one of his signature dishes—grilled haddock with cilantro butter. He seasoned the fish with salt and pepper and then browned it outside on the grill. After allowing it to cool slightly, he transferred it to a pan indoors. He added coarsely chopped garlic then stirred in butter, lime juice, and cilantro. Abby found it to be quite tasty and complimented the chef.

For dessert, they split a pint of Ben & Jerry's, finishing every last bite as they caught the last two periods of a Boston Bruins game. Again, Thom was blown away by Abby's intricate knowledge of the sport. He was discovering how well their personalities gelled and could feel his attraction to her deepening. Perhaps when this infernal Landry case was closed, he'd do something about it.

On Sunday, they took a long walk around the marsh. Abby was pleased that Thom was finally opening up to her. He had always been so inaccessible on a personal level and she took it as a compliment when he spoke at length about what his life had been like in California. Though he omitted details about his late wife and daughter, he recounted visiting the Monterey Bay Aquarium and shopping in Cannery Row, which had been made famous by the classic John Steinbeck novel. Thom became particularly animated talking about the Mission Basilica—a restored eighteenth-century Spanish mission with a beautiful garden and eerie old graveyard. Abby was captivated by the details and found herself daydreaming about traveling abroad with him some day.

Neither of them was in the mood for seafood so they headed over to JD's Burger Company for a late lunch/ early dinner. Thom had always been oddly amused by the restaurant's slogan: "flippin' good burgers." You could choose from a wide variety of cheeses, fixings, and buns to build your own little masterpiece. Thom remarked that even a naked burger was so thick you practically had to unhinge your jaw to fit one in your mouth. Since he had been covering their meal expenses for days now, Abby insisted on paying this time around. Thom joked that, had he known she was bankrolling the meal, he'd have chosen the Ocean House in Dennisport, which was notoriously expensive.

The day ended with them reading quietly in a cozy sitting area adjacent to Thom's living room. It was equipped with a fireplace and a bank of windows overlooking the marsh. Thom had started a book on ancient history, among his favorite topics, while Abby professed a weakness for cheesy medical yarns. She was halfway through a thriller about a super-virus that threatens the world's population. Abby read until she could barely keep her eyes open then excused herself to the guest house. Under different circumstances, she might have considered this an ideal weekend.

Lying in bed later on, Thom's thoughts drifted back to the reality of the Landry murder. There were so many unanswered questions—so many stones left unturned and the case was standing in the way of a life-altering decision. He resigned himself to bring matters to a swift conclusion so he could pursue a romantic relationship with Abby.

2

Immediately upon arriving at the station on Monday morning, Burroughs was greeted by Detective Barber who flooded him with information about Suzuki GSX owners in the Bay area.

"Okay, Fred, slow down. Let me get settled in here."

Like a kid vying for the attention of a parent, Barber followed Burroughs into his office and kept up an ongoing dialog.

"There were a lot of matches statewide," the Detective said eagerly, "but only a couple of dozen within fifty miles of the murder site. Out of those, only one bike was yellow."

Outstanding, thought Burroughs. "So who does it belong to?" He asked.

Barber dropped a photocopied license and registration on the desk. The papers landed on top of Burroughs' coffee. "Oh, sorry, Chief," he said, looking rather embarrassed. It was clear he hadn't had this much excitement on the job in a while.

Burroughs moved his coffee, obtained from the vending machine in the front lobby, to a safer location and examined the material in front of him. "Hmm," he said. "This doesn't match the description I was given."

"Description?" Barber said quizzically.

"Yeah," Burroughs replied. "There've been a few new developments. When I get a chance, I'll bring you up to speed. This is nice work, Fred. I think we might have a solid lead here."

"Thanks, Chief," Barber replied, glowing with the compliment.

The owner of the bike lived in Somerset which was located just above Fall River on Narragansett Bay.

"Can you get me this guy's phone number? I'd like to speak to him."

"I'm on it," Barber said dutifully, disappearing in haste.

Burroughs studied the license and registration. Pullman had described the cyclist as being tall and stocky with facial scars and a dusky complexion. Landry's secretary had provided identical details about the man who had caused a disturbance up in Plymouth. The guy in the driver's license photo was clearly not the same person. His name was Kevin Moore, a short, middle-aged man with a doughy face.

Barber came lumbering back into Burroughs' office with a yellow sticky note in his hand. He was slightly out of breath from his exertions. "I got the number, Chief."

"Great," said Burroughs, pasting the note to his desk blotter. "Don't go too far. I'm going to make this call and then I may have some more busywork for you."

"Okay , I'll be in my office."

Burroughs used his landline to dial Moore's number. A gruff voice answered after several rings.

"Good morning," Burroughs offered politely, "am I speaking to Kevin Moore?"

"Yeah, and if you're a telemarketer, I'm not buying anything."

"Mr. Moore, this is Chief Thom Burroughs with the Sandwich Police Department. I understand that you're the owner of a yellow Suzuki GSX motorcycle."

"That's right. What's this about?"

"We have reason to believe that your bike was involved in a crime here."

"What kind of crime?"

"I'm not at liberty to discuss the details. But I can tell you that it was quite serious."

"When did it take place?"

"A few days ago."

"Then you've got the wrong guy," Moore asserted. "I keep that bike at my summer cottage in Yarmouth. I haven't been there in over a month."

"I'm not accusing you of anything," Burroughs assured the man. "I'm just trying to gather some information. Can you tell me when you last rode the bike?"

"Labor Day weekend. I was buttoning the cottage up for winter and decided to take it out one last time."

"Does anyone else have access to the vehicle?"

"No. In fact, my wife wants me to get rid of it—says I'm going to kill myself on it someday."

"How about the cottage, any friends or family staying there?"

"Not since July. My wife's sister comes down from Minnesota every year."

"I see," said Burroughs. "Well, it appears as if your bike may have been stolen. Is there any way you can meet me out in Yarmouth to verify that."

Moore was not enthused by the proposal. "You mean today?" He said brusquely.

"The sooner the better," Burroughs intoned.

"That's an hour drive if I break every speed limit from here to the Sagamore. I'm a foreman on a construction crew and we're in the middle of a major project. There's no way I can do it ... not today, anyway."

"I understand. Do you mind if I take a ride out there myself and have a look?"

There was an ambivalent pause.

"I guess so," Moore said finally. "Do you know where the place is?"

"Not exactly, but I've got GPS. The address is 1123 Willow Lane, right?"

"Yup. I keep my bike in the garage out back. There are windows on either side. If it's in there, you'll see it. It's under a tarp"

"Got it. Thanks for your cooperation, Mr. Moore. I'll get back to you as soon as I can."

"Hey, what'd you say your name was again?"

"Thom Burroughs. I'm the Chief of Police here in Sandwich."

"I hope you're wrong about this, Chief. That bike cost me over ten grand."

"I'll let you know," Burroughs said courteously. "Have a nice day."

"Yeah, right, you, too."

"Bye."

When the call was complete, Burroughs grabbed the photocopied pages from Randall Landry's appointment book and headed up the hall to Barber's office. He provided the Detective with a number of fresh details about the case, including a thumbnail version of Philip Pullman's death.

"I've been meaning to get to these for days," he said, handing the papers to Barber, "but something always comes up. I'm heading out to Yarmouth now to check on that motorcycle."

"Do you need backup?"

"No, I'm good. What I really need is for you to take a look at the stuff I just gave you."

"All right. What should I be looking for?"

"I don't know, anything hinky I guess. If something seems out of place, make a note of it. If a particular name grabs your attention, run a background check. The Landrys catered to New England's wealthiest clients. You may recognize a few. Make sure that whatever information you gather doesn't leave the building. Got it?"

"Of course, Chief. I'll be totally discreet."

"Good luck," Thom said, heading back to his office to grab his coat. It was only 8:30 and he was making progress already. Things were looking up.

3

Burroughs hopped on the Mid-Cape Highway and got off at Exit 8. He used his GPS to guide him from there to Willow Lane, which was actually located in South Yarmouth, a separate village on Nantucket Sound. The street was lined with stately summer homes that were conspicuously unoccupied at present. Burroughs figured that Kevin Moore must be doing pretty well in the construction business. His so-called "cottage" was at least twice the size of Burroughs' home on the marsh.

There wasn't anybody around so the Chief parked his Jeep in front and strolled boldly up the driveway into the backyard. A white privacy fence was covered with English ivy. It was an invasive species and Burroughs noted that it was beginning to encroach upon the neighbor's tree line. Moore needed to get after it or he'd likely be fielding complaints from whoever owned the house next door.

The garage had two bays and, as advertised, windows on both sides. They were adorned with decorative shutters. There was a flagstone patio equipped with an outdoor fireplace on the left. To the right, a grassy path led to a paved area in back designated for garbage. Burroughs' attention was instantly drawn to a missing pane of glass on the patio-side window. Jagged shards around the grille suggested a break-in. The sill was heavily scored, indicating that someone had tried to pry the frame open before smashing the glass.

Peering into the garage, Burroughs was surprised to discover the outline of a motorcycle beneath a gray canvas tarp.

Now that's strange, he thought.

Aside from the bike and a few scattered lawn tools, the building was empty. So what had been the purpose of the break-in? Had Moore misplaced his garage door opener at some point and forced his way in, or had there been some other item of value in there? Burroughs was about to place a call to Moore when he noticed the dried apricots on the ground. Switching gears, he dialed Lieutenant Carlson's number instead.

Carlson sounded characteristically abrupt when he answered. "What do you need, Chief?"

"I've got something you're going to want to see."

"Oh, really, where are you?"

"At a vacant summer home in South Yarmouth."

"What are you doing there?"

"Following a lead on that yellow motorcycle."

"I see. And what exactly is it that I'm going to find so interesting?"

"I'm pretty sure our guy was here recently. There are pieces of dried fruit all over the ground."

"You've definitely got my attention. Shoot me the address and stay put. I'll be out there shortly."

***

The lieutenant arrived about forty minutes later accompanied by an evidence technician who he didn't bother to introduce. The guy looked like he was fresh out of college and had various nervous mannerisms. His eyes darted busily about the scene. Whenever he focused on a particular object, he blinked dramatically as if he were taking a mental picture of it. Burroughs found it a little odd.

The Chief ushered Carlson and his quirky assistant up the driveway into the yard, briefing them on the way. He showed them the broken window and damaged sill on the side of the garage. Carlson was perplexed by the scenario.

"I don't get it, the window's been tampered with, but the bike's still here. What the hell was our guy up to?"

"I don't know," said Burroughs. "Maybe he borrowed the bike then brought it back."

"To cover his tracks," Carlson proposed. "In that case, he'd have had another vehicle ... or an accomplice."

"True," Burroughs agreed.

"Have you been inside the garage yet?"

"I was waiting for you. One of us will have to open the window and crawl through."

"No need to go to that kind of trouble," said Carlson, turning to his assistant. "Somers, open the garage door for us, would you?"

As instructed, the tech pulled a small device from his pocket that resembled a handheld video game. He pressed a couple of buttons and the door responded.

"We call it 'Open Sesame,'" Carlson explained. "It uses a fixed code system for communicating with automatic garage door openers. It was created with the same components as a children's toy that was discontinued. Kids used the technology for wireless text messaging. Now felons and CSI units use it to break into people's garages."

Carlson fixed Burroughs with a smug look. "Pretty cool, huh?"

"You guys literally have all the toys," said Burroughs.

Somers stuffed the device back into his pocket and took a few steps into the garage. "I assume you'll want me to check the bike for latent prints," he said to Carlson.

"Of course," the lieutenant replied. "So where's this dried fruit?" He asked Burroughs.

"Behind the garage. I'll show you."

A concrete slab had been poured in back to accommodate garbage cans and firewood, which was stacked haphazardly against the building. Pieces of the fruit had been accidentally dropped or deliberately tossed into the grass beyond.

"Looks like our guy spent a little time back here," Carlson observed.

"Waiting for his ride, maybe," added Burroughs.

The lieutenant had a befuddled look on his face.

"This doesn't make sense," he said. "Guy returns the motorcycle to its rightful owner then drops evidence all over the ground just like he did out at the overlook. Too bad the previous batch of evidence didn't help us any."

"I thought you said you were able to get some DNA from it."

"We were. But when we ran it through our system, the results were skewed."

"How so?"

"Well, the DNA was a match for a terrorist named Abdullah Rashid. He had ties to Al Qaeda and was believed to be responsible for attacks against numerous U.S. installations overseas. At one point, he was detained at Guantanamo Bay, but ended up being released with a bunch of other suspects."

"Wow," said Burroughs.

"No kidding," Carlson continued. "We were getting ready to call in the Department of Homeland Security when we stumbled upon a rather puzzling fact. Rashid was killed in a 2010 Predator missile attack on his home in Iraq. The death was confirmed by high-ranking U.S. officials."

"Interesting," Burroughs remarked. "So how does the DNA of a notorious terrorist turn up at a murder site in Sandwich more than five years after his death?"

"If you figure it out, you can have my job," said Carlson. "No matter how sophisticated a system is, there are bound to be errors and anomalies. Nothing's perfect, right?"

"I guess so," Burroughs agreed.

Carlson's attention was suddenly drawn to the far end of the yard. "Hey, is that a white van back there?"

Beyond the privacy fence, Burroughs spotted an early model cargo van parked beside a neighboring garage. "I believe it is," he confirmed.

"I'll be damned," said Carlson.

They strolled to the edge of the yard where a horseshoe pit was situated parallel to the fence. Burroughs noted that the insidious English ivy was starting to choke out everything back here, too. The van was an old Chevy Express with rust along the wheel wells and undercarriage. Burroughs figured it had to be from the late 90s or early 2000s.

"So what are we looking at here?" The Chief wondered.

"One of Douglas Landry's neighbors spotted a white van idling in front of his house on the night he died."

"I thought the cause of death was listed as a heart attack."

"Yeah, the coroner in Weston thought so. But we'd be fools to believe that two Landry deaths in such a short span is anything less than suspicious. We're pretty sure our scarecrow killer borrowed a motorcycle from this property. If he knew how to hotwire a bike, it wouldn't be much of a stretch for him to boost the neighbor's van. Some of the older models can be started with a screwdriver. Our perp couldn't have chosen a better area to target. There isn't an occupied house within a quarter mile."

"You're right," Burroughs agreed. "I'll hop the fence and check it out."

"You do that," Carlson said with a touch of humor. "I'll wait for you on this side."

Burroughs wasn't as spry as he used to be, but he did keep in shape by walking around the marsh. The regular exercise provided him with enough agility to make it over the fence in a single awkward bound. The impact of the landing sent a shock wave that traveled from his ankles to his knees. Damn, thought Burroughs. I'm definitely feeling my age today.

One look inside the van confirmed Carlson's suspicions.

"The door's unlocked and there are loose ignition wires underneath the steering column."

"That's what I figured," said Carlson. "I'll have my guy check the van for prints, too. Hopefully, we'll come up with something we can use."

It was wishful thinking.

Despite his painstaking efforts, Somers was unable to lift an intact print from either vehicle, though he did confirm that both had been driven recently. Burroughs and Carlson concluded that the perp had likely worn gloves then wiped the vehicles clean for good measure. The presence of dried fruit continued to confound them. Why go to the trouble of returning stolen property and removing fingerprints while carelessly leaving DNA evidence at the scene?

With the theft of the motorcycle more or less established, the presence of the hot-wired van in proximity raised serious doubts about the nature of Douglas Landry's death. Carlson outlined a plan of action for his team. First, Landry's neighbor needed to be questioned along with whoever owned the van. If the neighbor turned out to be a credible witness and the van hadn't been tampered with by its owner, then a re-examination of Landry's body could be ordered to rule out foul play. In the meantime, the latest batch of dried fruit would be subjected to DNA analysis. With any luck, the results would prove helpful this time around.

Burroughs informed the lieutenant that Landry's appointment book was currently under review and promised to share any important findings. For the first time, he felt as if they were on the verge of a major breakthrough.

4

The New York operative showed up shortly before noon prayer, known as *Dhuhr*, with materials obtained from a supply depot in Stockbridge. The explosives arrived in two rented trucks after *Asr*, the late-afternoon observance. The man with the scars was immensely satisfied. Not only were the necessary resources safely in hand, but his force had grown significantly. There were now ten *jihadists* at his disposal.

Al-hamdu lillah!

Members of the newly assembled unit were not formally introduced to one another nor did they use their birth names. It was important to keep identities between groups confidential. Since his reputation preceded him, the man with the scars was treated with great respect. Everyone referred to him as Mullah, a name commonly bestowed upon clerics or mosque leaders.

The facilities at Stage Harbor were more than adequate to meet their needs. The lighthouse was no longer in service and the land had fallen into private hands. Like most outlying areas of the Cape, it was utterly deserted this time of year. A massive storage barn offered plenty of space to accommodate the trucks. The light keeper's house would provide shelter for the group until the event was underway.

Though the man with the scars hated America and the corrupt values it stood for, he was often impressed by its natural beauty. Forbidding mountains and parched deserts dominated the landscape of his homeland. In stark contrast, he found the ocean inspiring. He enjoyed watching the waves meet the shoreline in a violent and transitory embrace. It reminded him of life's ephemeral nature.

5

At the Sandwich Police Station, Burroughs was growing increasingly restless. Though the morning had been highly productive, the afternoon passed without any news from Carlson. Barber's examination of the appointment book, though still in progress, hadn't produced any viable leads so the Chief was forced to divert his attention back to everyday matters.

Mayor Jerzowicz had called inquiring about a game plan for Halloween and a sizeable stack of reports awaited Burroughs' review. He plowed laboriously through the paperwork then placed a courtesy call to the mayor, assuring him that patrols would be beefed up on the thirty-first to keep pace with all the pranksters who would inevitably be roaming the streets of Sandwich.

By 4:30, the Chief decided his services were no longer required and left for the day. Until very recently, he had been known to loiter at the station well into the evening to avoid the pervasive silence of his home. He had seriously considered getting a dog but realized that it was no substitute for human company, regardless of what passionate canine lovers had to say on the topic. Abby's extended visit had filled a void in his life. In fact, he actually found himself whistling as he crossed the parking lot to his Jeep.

There was nothing planned for dinner so Burroughs figured he would grab some Chinese food and invite Abby to join him. He was halfway to the restaurant when she called.

"Hey, Chief, don't start anything for dinner. I'm going to grab some takeout from the Golden Place in Bourne. Do you like General Tao's Chicken and fried dumplings?"

"They're two of my favorite things," he told her, astounded at how they always seemed to be on the same wavelength.

"Great. Are you still at work?"

"No. I'm on my way home."

"Yeah, me, too. Hey, remember all that bragging you did about your Scrabble expertise while we were walking around the marsh yesterday?"

"I wasn't bragging," he insisted.

"Yes you were and it was shameless. So now I'm serving you notice. After we get done eating, I'm going to kick your butt."

"You think you can beat me at Scrabble? I should warn you that many have been weighed in the balances and found wanting."

"Oh, it's on now, Chief."

"Bring it," he said with a chuckle.

"Careful what you wish for," she countered, ending the call.

And that's exactly how their evening went. After finishing every bite of the Chinese food, they engaged in a friendly but competitive Scrabble marathon that lasted until it was time for bed. By then, they had battled to a draw. Abby teased him about being "found wanting" while Thom pointed out that her projected "butt-kicking" had been an epic fail.

"There's always next time," she said as she lingered at the door to the carport.

"Do you want me to walk you out?" He offered.

"No, it's okay," she declined. "I know the way."

"All right, call me if you get lost," he said, feeling a strong urge to wrap his arms around her. He had never been good at deciphering female body language so he let the opportunity, if indeed there was one, slip away. "See you bright and early," he said instead.

"Not if I see you first," she joked.

As he watched her walk out the door, he realized two things: They hadn't discussed the Landry case all evening and, he was definitely falling for Abby.

6

In the morning, Thom and Abby ate breakfast together. There was no time for an elaborate meal, so they each had a quick cup of coffee with toasted raisin bread. Thom had taken the long walk down the driveway to fetch the newspaper and they divided it between them. Thom perused the sports section while Abby checked out the regional news. They read in contented silence, making occasional comments when something seemed worth sharing. The arrangement felt very comfortable to Abby—like an old married couple. For a fleeting instant last night, it had appeared as if Thom was going to add a little passion to the mix, but he had held back, likely out of respect for her. He was a true gentleman and she liked that about him. On the other hand, she would have welcomed his advances and wondered when he was going to take their relationship to another level. The chemistry between them was palpable. She resigned herself to let him walk her out to the guest house next time.

That ought to send a clear message, she thought.

At 7:45, they headed to their respective vehicles to begin the morning commute. Thom reminded her that his services were just a phone call away. Abby wished him a good day and warned him to be careful on the job. All the way to work she thought about how nice it would have been if she and Thom had called in sick together.

***

Abby spent the early part of the morning in her lab organizing files and taking inventory. Though a number of her peers found this aspect of the job rather irksome, she welcomed the busywork. There was almost always a dramatic reduction in cases this time of year and the downtime drove her to distraction.

She was preparing to fill out a monthly expense report when her cell phone rang, breaking the silence. She had recently switched ringtones and the new one, a retro chime, took her a little off guard.

"This is Doctor Rhodes."

"Hey, Abby, it's Kelley from the clinic."

"Hi, Kelley—how are you?"

"I'm fine. Well, actually I'm not. I really hate to bother you at work, but I've got a bit of a problem here and I need to pick your brain."

Abby knew something was wrong the second she heard Kelley's voice. Kelley took great pride in her ability to run the clinic independently and would never have called during business hours unless it was a matter of great importance.

"You're fine," Abby assured her. "I'm happy to help. What's going on?"

"Well, I was doing a med check and discovered that there are some injectables missing. I wouldn't have brought it to your attention if it were a case of a few seasonal flu shots being unaccounted for. This is a little more serious, I'm afraid."

"I see," Abby said gravely. "What's missing, Kelley?"

"In addition to a needle-free injector, a five-milliliter bottle of potassium chloride and several units of Pavulon."

It took a few seconds for Abby to fully grasp the significance of Kelley's dilemma. The first drug was used to boost potassium levels in the blood, particularly in older patients who have suffered through prolonged bouts of diarrhea. The latter drug, also known as pancuronium bromide, was a muscle relaxant typically used with general anesthesia to help facilitate the intubation process. Emergencies requiring intubation were rarely dealt with at the clinic, but materials necessary to carry out the procedure were kept on hand in limited supply. While neither of the missing drugs was overtly hazardous if taken by itself in a standard dose, a combination of the two would almost certainly prove fatal. Abby was eminently aware that both medications were used to execute death row prisoners in conjunction with a third drug known as sodium pentothal—a fast-acting barbiturate. Without the last ingredient, the injection would be agonizingly painful. The implications of the scenario were disturbing. Perhaps someone had been planning a grisly suicide. Or a murder.

"Who has access to the med closet?" Abby inquired, making a concerted effort to sound calm.

"The PA's and doctors, including myself, have their own keys. The nurses all share a copy."

"Where do they keep it?"

"In the nurses' station. It's on a lanyard. Sometimes they wear it around their necks."

Abby was familiar with the entire medical staff and none of them struck her as being particularly suspicious.

"Who else has access to the nurses' station?"

"Well, we have a custodian of course," Kelley said after giving it some thought. "He works second shift. He's been with us for a couple of years. In fact, I believe you've met him before."

Abby tried to produce an image in her mind but came up empty.

"Maybe," she said. "I don't remember him. So have you questioned anyone yet?"

"No. It's a sensitive topic and I wasn't sure how to proceed. That's why I called looking for advice."

"You're sure the drugs were on hand?"

"Yeah, I'm positive. I signed off on them during my last med count on Friday morning. There's no record of them having been administered."

There was a brief pause as Abby considered the best course of action.

"Well, I know your entire staff aside from this janitor. He'd be the first person I'd talk to if I were you. I'd be happy to sit in if you're uncomfortable."

"No, I'm okay with it," Kelley asserted. "But there may be a problem. I just remembered, he put in his resignation a few weeks ago. Friday was his last day."

***

The conversation with Kelley warranted an immediate call to Thom. Abby rehashed the particulars with him, emphasizing the devastating effects of the medications if administered together. With that having been established, she reiterated her suspicions about Douglas Landry's death.

"You think the missing drugs were used to kill him?" Thom said, astonished by the possibility.

"I can't prove it at the moment, but I'm pretty sure, yeah. There's no logical reason for those drugs to turn up missing. You can't re-sell them on the street and they have almost no therapeutic value to the average person. But to anyone planning a murder, they'd be ideal. Pavulon paralyzes the muscles while potassium chloride stops the heart. In the absence of a toxicology screening, any coroner would determine the cause of death to be a heart attack. The other missing item, a needle-free injector, would offer the killer a distinct advantage. It's easier to handle and there's hardly any tissue damage to draw suspicion from investigators later on."

"So tell me more about this janitor," Thom prompted her.

"Well, apparently his name is Michael Kinney. The director told me he's been working at the clinic for a couple of years and that I've met him before. The funny thing is, I have absolutely no recollection of it. I keep trying to picture a face in my mind but end up drawing a blank. Isn't that strange?"

"Not really," Thom remarked. "If I've learned one thing in my line of work, it's that memory is a faulty device. Just because you were introduced to this guy doesn't mean that you'd be able to consciously remember it, especially after enough time has passed."

"I guess. But in my line of work, I'm supposed to have a head for details."

"Don't sell yourself short, Doc. You've got a great head on your shoulders. Do you know the guy's address?"

"Yeah, I had the director look it up. According to the information in his personnel file, he lives at 134 Old Cedar Street in South Yarmouth. He's in apartment 11B."

"South Yarmouth, that's interesting. I was just out there yesterday following a lead," he told her.

"Really, anything helpful?"

"I don't know … maybe. It's kind of up in the air. I'll share the details with you later. Right now I need to see about this Kinney guy. This is big, Abby. It might be the break we were looking for."

"I really hope so," she said, "because I'd like to close this chapter of my life and move on."

It was pretty clear to Thom that she was talking about more than the Landry case.

"That makes two of us," he told her.

7

As soon as he hung up with Abby, Burroughs placed a call to Carlson. The lieutenant wasn't answering so he decided to handle the situation alone. He knew he should give the police in South Yarmouth a heads-up first, especially since he had meandered into their jurisdiction yesterday. But Burroughs knew the desk sergeant there all too well. A prickly little man by the name of Frank Daulton, he would almost certainly balk at the prospect of letting an outsider tread on his rightful territory. The Chief had learned long ago that, in order to get things done, you had to break with standard protocol from time to time. Daylight was burning. And the leads in the Landry case weren't getting any fresher.

Annie was working dispatch until 3:30. Burroughs notified her of his departure then hopped in his Jeep, heading toward the Mid-Cape Highway. The trip would normally have taken about a half hour, but he really put the pedal down this time. He reached the outskirts of South Yarmouth in a little over twenty minutes. Aside from the Bass River and the beaches on Nantucket Sound, there wasn't much in the way of tourist attractions here. There were a handful of popular restaurants and hotels, but other than that, the town was mostly residential.

Burroughs programmed his GPS for 134 Old Cedar Street, which was an apartment complex that had once served as an elementary school. Most of the brick facade had been covered with vinyl siding and he didn't like it. Why convert an old school into living space without preserving the character of the original structure? he thought.

The parking spots were sparsely occupied this time of day with most tenants presumably at work. Burroughs followed a series of signs around back where the B-suites were located. The outside entrance wasn't locked and he entered the building undeterred. Unlike the altered exterior, the inside hallway retained its original look with shiny tiled floors and whitewashed brick walls. Even the drinking fountains and fire alarm stations remained. The apartment doors had opaque wired glass with numbers stenciled on them. There were six suites on the main floor. Burroughs figured 11B must be on the upper level so he took the nearest stairwell, his footfalls echoing loudly.

11B was situated at the end of the hall. Burroughs loitered beside the door—listening. In a nearby apartment, a television was tuned to a morning game show. He could hear the host prattling on about a showroom full of fabulous prizes. There were no discernible noises coming from 11B. Perhaps Michael Kinney wasn't home or maybe he was sleeping.

Instinctively, Burroughs unfastened the safety snap on his holster before rapping loudly on the door. His heart was hammering in his chest as he waited for a response. He counted to ten then knocked again, more insistently this time. The seconds stretched into minutes without a reply. Disappointed, he weighed his options.

It was a considerable drive from Sandwich to South Yarmouth and Burroughs didn't want to walk away empty-handed. He tried the door and found it unlocked. Though it was an egregious violation of the inhabitant's privacy, he poked his head inside the apartment.

The floor plan was completely open with no separation between the kitchen, dining area or living room. A door at the far end of the flat ostensibly led to a private bath. Michael Kinney was apparently unconcerned with material possessions. The walls were completely devoid of art. Aside from an old farmhouse table, a cheap futon and a veneer wood desk, there was no furniture. A pair of plastic milk crates served as an entertainment center.

"Hello," Burroughs addressed the empty space, "anybody home?"

Nothing.

He noted that the desk was littered with papers and photos. Examining them without a warrant would be considered an illegal search, but since he had fractured several rules already, he figured he may as well go for broke here. He crossed the room with his right hand hovering cautiously near his holster. The door on the far wall was ajar with darkened space looming beyond. Anyone lurking in the shadows would undoubtedly be aware of his presence.

Keeping the partially open door in his periphery, Burroughs had a look at the items on the desk. There were U.S. roadmaps with specific locations circled in red pen. A laptop was buried beneath a pile of notes scribbled in a foreign hand. Burroughs was no expert, but the letters appeared to be of Middle Eastern origin. There were pictures of lighthouses scattered about and he recognized all of them, most notably Nauset Light, which was located in Eastham. Photos of two major New England bridges were also included amongst the jumble of information. Burroughs easily identified them as the Bourne and the Sagamore. The Bourne was an arched bridge with a suspended deck connecting Cape Cod to mainland Massachusetts via Route 6. The Sagamore carried four lanes of traffic across the Cape Cod Canal on Route 28, providing freeway connections from I-495 and I-195.

Burroughs was flustered and a little distressed by the material. He was mulling over possible explanations when he was struck in the head from behind. The entire room made a full revolution before going completely black.

8

It was turning out to be a very trying day for Lieutenant Carlson. A phone call to the coroner's office in Weston had produced discouraging news. Douglas Landry's body had been released to a funeral home in Dover where the embalming process had been completed. As if that weren't enough to rattle the lieutenant's chain, a lab tech had just informed him that the DNA evidence collected from South Yarmouth had been cross-contaminated with the original sample. It was the only practical explanation for the latest set of anomalous results. The alternative scenario, a dead terrorist stalking the dunes of Sandwich in a scarecrow costume, was highly implausible.

Carlson leaned back in his desk chair and rubbed his temples. He had been making a concerted effort to reduce his caffeine intake lately and it was causing him debilitating headaches. They were the kind that pain relievers couldn't touch. With the Landry investigation fraying his nerves, he decided it might be best to grab a Red Bull or a Mountain Dew. If he didn't, he was liable to take a swing at someone. On his way out the door, a troubling thought struck him.

No one had ever checked back with Doctor LaMoyne, the guy who had talked to the scarecrow at the hospital fundraiser in Harwich. Carlson had meant to delegate the task but had gotten hopelessly sidetracked. At the moment, LaMoyne was their only material link to the killer and it was well worth a follow-up. Cursing himself for being so disorganized, he headed back to his desk to retrieve the contact information.

His caffeine fix could wait.

<h1 style="text-align:center">9</h1>

Aaban pulled his vehicle, an aging Kia Optima, into a mini-mart on Route 28 and braced himself for the impending unpleasantness. Though he was certain his superior would be furious about how he had handled the incident in the apartment, it was a conversation that needed to take place sooner rather than later. Time was of the essence now.

The number to Mullah's current burner phone was written on a piece of scrap paper in the glove compartment. Aaban fished it out and placed the dreaded call, anticipating the worst. His hands were shaking noticeably.

"Hello. Who is this?"

"It's me, Aaban."

"Did you clear the items out of the apartment like I told you to?"

"Yes. But there was an unexpected problem."

"What problem?"

"A police officer arrived shortly after I did."

"I hope you weren't foolish enough to speak to him."

"Of course not. But the door was unlocked and he let himself in."

"Did he see you?"

"I don't think so. I stayed out of sight for as long as he could until I noticed him looking at our plans. Then I was forced to intervene."

"What did you do?"

"I knocked him unconscious. Then I grabbed everything I could carry and left."

"So you have the laptop and the notes?"

"Yes."

"Good. Did you check the policeman for ID?"

"I did. His name is Thom Burroughs. He's the one protecting Doctor Rhodes."

"This definitely complicates things," Mullah said petulantly.

As the conversation lapsed into sullen silence, Aaban grew increasingly anxious about the consequences he might face. He had seen Mullah administer vile punishments for even the smallest transgressions and those punishments were almost always meted out in front of peers. Though Aaban had absolutely no fear of death, he shuddered at the prospect of being publicly humiliated.

"Are you certain the policeman saw our plans?"

"Yes, but only briefly. I doubt he was able to translate them."

"True," Mullah agreed, "He'll still need to be dealt with as soon as possible."

"I understand," Aaban said, greatly relieved that Mullah was keeping his volatile temper in check. "How would you like to handle it?"

"We'll use the woman as bait."

10

Lieutenant Carlson was rarely surprised by anything, but when Doctor LaMoyne promptly returned his call, he chalked it up as a highly unusual occurrence. Most doctors kept busy schedules and considered themselves to be above the banalities of law enforcement.

"Thanks for getting back to me so soon," Carlson offered politely, finishing the last swig of Mountain Dew. He could feel his headache subsiding.

"No problem," the Doctor replied. "What can I help you with?"

"One of my officers spoke to you last week about a fundraiser you attended in Harwich. I'm just following up. Do you mind if I ask a few questions?"

"Sure," said LaMoyne. "But we'll have to keep it brief. I have a consult in about ten minutes."

"No problem. This shouldn't take long," Carlson assured him. "So how did you know Randall Landry?"

"We ran some educational workshops together at Beth Israel Hospital in Boston. I helped him publish his first paper in the *American Journal of Cosmetic Surgery*."

"Did you know each other outside of work?"

"Yes. We were members of the same country club. We played golf together fairly often during the summer."

"So you knew him well."

"I guess so," LaMoyne conceded.

"Do you know of anyone who had an ax to grind with him?"

"You mean serious enough to kill him?"

"Whatever," Carlson said.

There was a calculated silence as the Doctor chose his words carefully.

"Randall attained a level of success in the field that most people only dream of. He craved attention and usually got it wherever he went. I'm sure you can appreciate how that made some of his colleagues envious."

"What about people outside the medical profession?" Carlson pressed. "Any jealous husbands or disgruntled patients?"

LaMoyne chuckled sourly. "There were jealous husbands, sure. But you don't need me to tell you that. You can read all about it in the tabloids."

"What about his patients, any dissatisfied customers?"

"Like I said, Randall was a leader in the field. The only surgeon who came close to matching his skill set was his father. I watched one of their joint procedures and it was uncanny. I've never seen that kind of precision before or since. Then again, you're always going to have patients who are difficult to please."

"Name one," Carlson prodded.

"I'm not sure I'm at liberty to discuss the topic," said LaMoyne guardedly. "I assume you've heard of a thing called the doctor-patient privilege."

"Are we talking about one of your own patients?"

"No, I suppose not."

"Then the privilege doesn't apply."

Carlson was tiring quickly of the Doctor.

"There was an individual who approached me after a series of procedures Randall had performed," LaMoyne divulged. "He was extremely unhappy with Landry's work and kept referring to him as a quack."

"When was this?"

"A couple of years ago. The procedures had left the man with some noticeable facial scars and he wanted me to fix them. He offered me cash, which I found to be highly irregular. Randall's father had assisted with the surgeries and, given the extent of their efforts, I considered the scars to be an acceptable contingency. I refused the case."

"Had the guy been in a car accident or something?"

"No, that's the kicker. The surgery was elective. The man had undergone a complete facial reconstruction."

"I don't imagine there are many doctors who would sign on for something like that," Carlson assumed.

"You're right," LaMoyne confirmed. "It's delicate work, to say the least. And scars are inevitable. In this case, they were along the patient's jawline."

"What was the patient's name?"

"I'm not sure I'm comfortable releasing that information," LaMoyne wavered.

"Would you be more comfortable releasing it after I've taken you into custody?" Carlson proposed icily.

There was an awkward pause.

"Kinney," grumbled LaMoyne. "His name was Michael Kinney."

11

Burroughs awoke in pain. As the room swam slowly back into focus, he checked his head for blood. There wasn't any, but a sizeable lump was throbbing uncomfortably. He tried to work himself to a sitting position and, as he did, pinpoints of white light darted before his eyes. Grasping for his holster, he was pleased to discover that the Glock was still in his possession. How long have I been out? he wondered.

On the kitchen counter, a coffee maker with a digital time display gave him an approximate answer. He had arrived in town shortly before noon. Assuming the clock was accurate, it was now 1:05. His assailant had clobbered him pretty good.

Within a few minutes, he had regained his senses and was able to stand without experiencing dizziness or nausea. Aside from a splitting headache and a nasty bump, he felt okay. Someone had removed all of the pictures and notes from the desk while he was unconscious. The laptop was missing, too, which could only mean that it contained sensitive information. The pictures of regional landmarks along with the maps and notes scribbled in Middle Eastern text suggested some sort of terrorist scheme. What on Earth had Kinney been plotting here? The man was obviously a menace and needed to be taken into custody posthaste.

Burroughs pulled out his phone and dialed Carlson. His call was instantly transferred to voice mail. He wondered what was keeping the lieutenant so busy. Perhaps there were new developments in the case. If so, Burroughs doubted they were more significant than what he had stumbled upon here in South Yarmouth.

Burroughs placed another call to the station in Sandwich. His Jeep was not equipped with a mobile computer and he needed information that might lead him to Kinney's current whereabouts.

"Sandwich Police Department. How may I assist you?"

"Annie, it's Thom. I need to speak to Fred."

"Sure, Chief, I'll patch you through to him. Hey, while I've got you on the line, have you made out the schedule for Halloween yet? The guys have all been asking about it."

"Dammit," Burroughs muttered.

With everything going on, he had completely forgotten that tomorrow was Halloween.

"I haven't finished it yet," he said apologetically. "Tell them I'll post it by the end of my shift today."

"Will do, Chief, thanks. I'll transfer you over to Freddie now."

There was scarcely a pause before the Detective picked up, sounding eager to please.

"This is Detective Barber. What can I help you with?"

"Fred, it's Thom. I need you to drop whatever you're doing and check the system for information on a guy named Michael Kinney. He lives in South Yarmouth."

Burroughs could hear Barber jotting the information down.

"You got it Chief. Should I call you back or do you want to hold?"

"I'll hold."

"Okay. I'll try to be as quick as possible."

"The quicker the better, Fred."

"All right, sit tight."

Burroughs held the phone to his ear while he searched Kinney's apartment for more contraband. The desk drawers were empty except for a few unused envelopes and miscellaneous office supplies. The plastic milk crates serving as a TV stand were cluttered with books and DVDs, all of them dealing with the subject of Islam. What appeared to be a prayer mat was rolled up neatly in the corner of the room. It was clear that Kinney was a devoted Muslim. But labeling him a terrorist based on the items currently in his apartment would be a quantum leap. Burroughs wished there had been more time to survey the material that had been removed.

Barber returned to the phone with some interesting results.

"Looks like your guy's a ghost, Chief. He's got no criminal record, doesn't have a driver's license, and isn't registered to vote. There's no current phone number, either. He's had that South Yarmouth address for a couple of years now, but there's nothing on file before then. I know that's not much to go on. Sorry. What'd this guy do, anyway?"

"I'm more concerned with what he might be planning for the future," Burroughs answered cryptically. "I'll be back in Sandwich in about half an hour. Keep searching the database."

"You got it, Chief," Barber said obligingly. "See you soon."

"Right. Bye, Fred."

As he ended the call, it occurred to Burroughs that he could get a full description of Kinney from Abby's contacts at the clinic in Hyannis. That would allow him to post an APB. He dialed her number and cursed aloud when it went straight to voicemail. Frustrated, he snapped his phone shut and left the apartment.

12

The Barnstable County Coroner's offices were located in Buzzard's Bay, a census-designated place in the town of Bourne with a square area of fewer than three miles. Abby shared the antiquated building with several other county officials, among them the assessor, auditor, and commissioner. Her lab was situated in the basement at the end of a long, gloomy corridor. Security measures were virtually nonexistent. Visitors could bypass the receptionist on the main floor through a service entrance that granted direct access to Abby's work area. While most modern medical facilities were equipped with swipe card entry systems and closed circuit cameras, Abby's lab was protected by a deadbolt and an archaic intercom. A peephole allowed her to see whoever was standing in proximity to the door. Aside from funeral directors and delivery men, she rarely received visitors anyway so security had never been an issue.

Abby was sterilizing her instruments when she heard the intercom buzz loudly. She wasn't expecting company and the sound startled her a little. Removing her latex gloves, she padded to the door and depressed the TALK button.

"Who is it?"

"I've got a package from Boston Scientific," a heavily accented voice replied.

The company was one of her top suppliers, but she hadn't placed an order this month.

"I'm not scheduled for any deliveries," she informed the courier. "What do you have for me?"

"I'm not sure, Ma'am. Let me check the invoice."

Abby peeked through the glass aperture and saw an olive-skinned man in a khaki delivery uniform struggling with a large and presumably heavy box. On impulse, she slid aside the deadbolt and opened the door. It was a major miscalculation. Within seconds, the man had his hands around her throat and had pinned her to one of the examination tables.

As she fought vainly to break free, a second man entered the room. Abby's attention was instantly drawn to the scars along his jawline. She recognized him from the clinic and wondered why she had been unable to recall his face earlier.

"Good afternoon, Doctor Rhodes," the man greeted her. "I believe we've met before."

13

Carlson sat alone in his office squeezing a foam stress ball while ruminating over the facts in the Landry case. A clearer picture of the crime was emerging though he lacked sufficient details to bring it into focus at present. The conversation with LaMoyne had prompted him to consider divergent theories.

Perhaps the DNA analysis of the dried fruit had been accurate after all. Perhaps Abdullah Rashid had been falsely listed among the casualties of a missile strike in Iraq. Carlson had heard of government reports being deliberately exaggerated to lull the American public into believing the U.S. was winning the war on terror.

If Rashid had indeed survived the attack, it was remotely possible that he had slipped into the States and enlisted the services of a renowned cosmetic surgeon to alter his physical appearance. This hypothesis came with a host of troubling questions. Assuming that Randall Landry and his father knew Rashid's identity, why had Rashid waited two years to dispose of them? What business did Rashid have in New England? And, was he operating alone or in conjunction with a sleeper cell?

A rudimentary search for information on Michael Kinney had yielded dubious results. Aside from a mailing address and social security number, the guy was off the grid. Carlson had assigned a full background check to one of his profilers then shifted his attention to the Global Terrorist Database. He learned that Rashid's wife and three sons had all been killed during the assault on their home which had taken place on October 31, 2010. By Carlson's estimation, that would leave Rashid with a serious vendetta against the U.S. government.

A knock on his office door disrupted the lieutenant's train of thought.

"Who is it?" He called brusquely.

"It's Aaron Petersen, sir. I'm the forensic accountant."

"Come in," Carlson prompted him.

A broad-shouldered man standing well over six feet tall, Pederson looked more like a football player than a bean counter.

"Have a seat," Carlson insisted. "I almost forgot about you. I expected a report by the end of last week."

"I know," said Pederson contritely. "Sorry, Lieutenant. They've got me working a bunch of cases at once."

"I understand," acknowledged Carlson. "So what did you find out about Randall Landry?"

"Well, for starters, he wasn't bankrupt—far from it in fact. As it turns out, he'd been receiving wire transfers from various sources for several months. At the time of his death, he'd accumulated close to four million dollars. There were no substantial debits in the last calendar year, either, which more or less debunks the theory that he was being blackmailed."

"Interesting," Carlson remarked. "So where was all the money coming from?"

"Offshore accounts mostly," said Pederson, placing a manila folder on Carlson's desk. "It's all there in my report."

Carlson picked up the folder and skimmed the first few pages. The most recent deposit had been made shortly before Randall's death. It had originated from a standard money market account belonging to Douglas Landry. Had Randall painted himself as a victim to extort money from his own father? Carlson found that rather odd.

"Any idea what the money was for?" He prodded.

"We have a working theory," Pederson explained. "A few years ago, Randall was involved in a series of ill-advised financial ventures. He lost a lot of money in his divorce and was probably looking to rebuild some capital. Though his credit had taken a serious hit, he tried to secure an eight-figure business loan with his father as co-applicant. Apparently, the plan was to open a series of cosmetic surgery practices all over New England with intent to eventually go national. But the bank wouldn't approve the loan due to Randall's shaky financial past. We assume that he began courting private investors to back his proposal at some point after that."

Carlson grunted. "Well, that opens up a whole new can of worms."

"It does," Pederson agreed. "Looks like you guys have your work cut out for you."

14

Aaban was growing weary of Mullah's irresponsible decisions. The event could just as easily have been staged during the holy month Ramadan, which had fallen during the heart of tourist season on Cape Cod. But Mullah had chosen the pagan holiday associated with the deaths of his immediate family members instead. While the attack on Mullah's home had been a grievous offense, Aaban felt that justice would have been better served during Ramadan, when the spiritual rewards were far greater.

The death of Randall Landry had been necessary. After all, he had come to Mullah seeking money in exchange for maintaining the secrecy of Mullah's identity. Under Islamic law, extortion was considered a capital offense and the doctor had gotten what he deserved. But the murders that followed had been reckless. With a little over ten hours still to go before the event, local police appeared to be closing in. And Mullah's latest scheme placed the entire operation in jeopardy.

As he climbed out of his vehicle and headed into the front lobby of the Sandwich Police Station, Aaban recited a silent prayer.

Subhanalla-thee sakh-khara-lana haatha wa-ma kun-na lahoo muqrineena wa inna ila Rabbina la-mun-qali-boon. Glory be to Allah who has brought this under our control though we are unable to control it. Sure, we are to return to our Lord.

Upon entering the building, Aaban instantly felt out of place. His long robe and colorful head scarf prompted a curious look from the woman at the front desk. He was sure they didn't get too many Muslims in here. The woman wasn't wearing a uniform or badge, which indicated to Aaban that she had no authority to detain him. There were no officers around at the moment either, which boosted his confidence a little.

"What can I do for you, sir?" The woman said in a voice that sounded as if she were nursing a cold.

"I have an important document for Chief Burroughs."

"He's currently out of his office. Is it something he needs to sign?"

"No Ma'am."

"Well, you can either have a seat in the lobby or leave it with me. I'll be sure to give it to him as soon as he gets in."

"That would be perfect, thank you," Aaban said cordially. He reached inside his robe and produced a plain white envelope and handed it to her.

The woman appraised the parcel suspiciously.

"Who should I say this is from?"

"A friend who wishes to remain anonymous."

With that, Aaban turned and walked quickly out of the lobby.

Mission accomplished.

15

Carlson was faced with a major dilemma—whether or not to contact the Department of Homeland Security. A conversation with his profiler had more or less confirmed the fact that there was no such person as Michael Kinney. The social security number associated with the name actually belonged to Hunter Tremblay, a nine-year-old boy currently residing in Reno, Nevada. The man posing as Kinney had likely appropriated the number for the purpose of finding and maintaining employment. It was a textbook move among illegal aliens.

There were at least two factors preventing Carlson from making the call to DHS. First and foremost, his reputation was on the line. Abdullah Rashid's DNA, or DNA close enough to be considered a statistical match, had been recovered from two separate crime scenes. But right now, all Carlson had was a far-flung theory involving a stolen identity, an unscrupulous cosmetic surgeon, and a falsified government intelligence report. He needed something a little less fantastic to avoid ending up as a punch line. Secondly, he loathed the idea of yielding to the Feds. He had expended a lot of time and energy on this investigation so far and he'd be damned if he was going to let a bunch of swaggering bureaucrats steal his thunder.

Carlson had stopped answering his cell phone shortly before lunch. On the off chance he had missed something important, he checked his recent calls. There were voice mails from his primary physician and financial advisor. Since neither was likely to be bearing good news, he ignored them. Scrolling further down the list, he noted that Burroughs had attempted to contact him a couple of hours ago. The Chief was turning out to be a surprising asset to the case and Carlson made a mental note to get back to him at some point. Right now, he needed another Mountain Dew. His headache had returned with a vengeance.

16

As Burroughs entered the lobby of the police station, Annie greeted him with atypical enthusiasm.

"Hey, Chief, some guy dropped off an envelope for you about fifteen minutes ago," she said excitedly.

"Really? Who was it?"

"I don't know. He looked like some kind of oil Sheik. He was dressed in a robe and a turban."

Ethnic diversity was sorely lacking on Cape Cod and the Chief was sometimes amazed by the tactlessness of the native population.

"Did he say what was in it?" Burroughs inquired, imagining a host of unpleasant scenarios.

"He said it was an important document. When I asked for his name, he told me he was a 'friend who wished to remain anonymous.' Those were his exact words."

"Well, let's have a look at it," said Burroughs. "I assume you've touched it?"

"Yeah," Annie replied, looking extremely apprehensive. "Should I have been wearing gloves?"

"Well, if there was anything toxic on the outside of the envelope, you'd probably be sick by now. But I can't vouch for what's inside until I see it."

Annie reached into her desk and grabbed the envelope. She handed it off to Burroughs as if it were a piece of hazardous waste. Being a standard white #10 business envelope, it was somewhat translucent. When Burroughs held it up to the light, he could see the contents. To his immense relief, there was no evidence of suspicious powder inside. It contained a 3 X 5 index card, on which a simple message had been printed in block letters: "CHECK YOUR EMAIL."

"So what's in it?" Annie asked fretfully.

Burroughs figured it would be safer for everyone involved if he kept the message to himself until he had determined the gravity of the situation.

"I can't say for sure," he lied, "but it does look like some sort of signed document. I'm sure it's nothing to worry about. I'll open it in my office."

Annie expelled a heavy sigh. "You really gave me a start. I was thinking about that anthrax scare they had at the post office in Dennis a few years ago."

"I remember that," Burroughs said. "You should never let your guard down. Don't ever forget that, Annie. It's important."

"Got it, Chief," she replied soberly.

Though Burroughs had originally planned on checking in with Detective Barber, the communication in the envelope commanded higher priority at the moment. He headed straight to his office and shut the door behind him.

The Chief had always prided himself on staying cool in crisis situations, but he was suddenly feeling overwhelmed. In addition to the latest twist in the Landry case, he still hadn't made out a shift schedule for tomorrow. In less than twenty-four hours, the town's most nefarious pranksters would be on the streets looking for trouble and restrictions on the amount of overtime allotted to county employees made assembling a sufficient Halloween staff a daunting task.

One step at a time, Burroughs reminded himself as he signed into his email account. He dreaded whatever unsavory surprise lay in store for him. He was certain it had something to do with the unpleasant incident out in South Yarmouth and he seriously doubted that his unknown assailant intended to let him off so easily after viewing the contents of Apartment 11B.

Burroughs' heart literally skipped a beat when he saw his most recent email. It had been sent from Abby's phone twenty minutes ago. He noted that it had a photo attachment and that the subject line read: "Help!" His pulse began to quicken as he clicked on the link.

The text was comprised of three ominous lines.

Come to the Stage Harbor lighthouse after dark. Speak to no one about this. Come alone or the doctor dies.

The attached photos turned his stomach. There were three pictures all taken in Abby's lab. In the first two, a brutish looking man with swarthy skin had his hands around Abby's throat. A piece of silver duct tape had been applied to her mouth and she was blindfolded. The man restraining her appeared to be wearing a UPS uniform. The last photo made Burroughs' blood run cold. It was a selfie taken by a man in a burlap mask. The mask had a crude smiley face painted on it.

17

Carlson slugged the last of his Mountain Dew and headed up the hall to meet with Walter Delacroix—his most reliable analyst. No one was more adept at evaluating the facts and arriving at practical conclusions. If there were insights to be drawn from the forensic accountant's report, Delacroix would promptly root them out.

A copious dose of caffeine had left Carlson with a cache of restless energy. He had gained a lot of weight over the years and moved with all the grace of a polar bear. Though his wife had been trying to get him to eat healthier for over a decade, he was addicted to fast food, sugary drinks, and powdered donuts. In spite of a daily dose of Lipitor, he was confident that his battle against triglycerides was a losing cause. Everyone died of something he often told himself. Some folks were better nourished when that day arrived.

Despite a dozen years of service, Delacroix had yet to move up in the ranks on account of his negligent social skills. A stereotypical office geek with thick glasses and a cowlick, he had a tendency to talk down to everyone, supervisors included. If not for his exceptional research abilities and eidetic memory, he would likely have been terminated long ago. His workstation was situated in a labyrinth of cubicles reserved for the lower-to-middle pay grades. Carlson found him at his computer scrolling through crime scene photos. He didn't even bother to look up from the monitor when Carlson entered his space.

"What do you need, Lieutenant?" Delacroix bristled, sounding bored and harassed.

No stranger to social ineptitude, Carlson brushed it off. "I've got a report I need you to look at. I promise it's more interesting than what you're working on right now."

Delacroix spun in his chair and faced Carlson. His greasy hair was matted to his forehead. His glasses were slightly askew, giving him a hapless look. "What is it?" he inquired impassively.

"It's a financial activity report."

"Really? I thought you said it was something interesting."

"It's from the Randall Landry case."

Intrigued, Delacroix raised an eyebrow. "All right, let's see it."

Carlson handed the folder to Delacroix. The analyst riffled through the pages, making throaty noises as he did. Carlson suspected that Delacroix was suffering from Asperger's or some other disorder within the autism spectrum. It's a wonder he had ever landed a job working around people.

"This is shady business," Delacroix commented after absorbing a majority of the report in less than three minutes. "Most of these deposits were third-party wire transfers from offshore accounts. That means the people who made them were serious about maintaining their anonymity. About a quarter of all offshore accounts are tied to white-collar crime, so there's an excellent chance that Doctor Landry was receiving funds from at least one corrupt source. What really stands out to me are the deposits made on August third and September fifth of this year. Both came from Sparbuch accounts."

"What are those?" Carlson inquired.

"The most clandestine accounts on the planet. They originate in Austria where banking laws prohibit the disclosure of client details to third parties. It's an imprisonable offense. The issuing bank doesn't keep any names or addresses on file and no statements are ever mailed out. All you need to open an account is an Austrian I.D. After that, you can send the bank your code word by registered mail asking that your funds be transferred to anywhere in the world. The only catch is that your money has to be converted into Austrian schillings. I've heard the exchange rates are excellent."

"So there's no way to trace who those deposits came from?"

"Nope," asserted Delacroix, taking off his glasses and wiping them on his argyle sweater vest. "Do you have any idea what Landry was up to?"

"Supposedly, he was looking to open a chain of cosmetic surgery practices and he needed investors."

"Well, he must have been desperate. I wouldn't be surprised if some of these deposits are tied to money laundering operations."

"Interesting," Carlson said. "Why don't you hang on to that report for a little while? See what you dig up."

Delacroix shrugged. "I've got a couple of other projects going. It wouldn't be my top priority."

Though he was trying to sound cool and detached, Carlson knew the man all too well and could tell that he wanted in badly.

"No problem," the lieutenant conceded. "Take your time. When you get a chance, we'll talk about it."

Delacroix nodded once then spun his chair back around, indicating to Carlson that their conversation was concluded. On the way back to his office, Carlson thought about how grand ambitions and greed had likely gotten Randall Landry killed.

18

Burroughs pulled his backup piece from the wall safe and strapped it to his belt. The weight of both guns felt awkward and would take some getting used to. He had filled his pockets with additional rounds in case things got really ugly. Though he had always held his own at the firing range, he had never been in an actual shootout. He hoped he could handle himself if the situation arose. Abby's life depended on it.

Checking his watch, Burroughs noted that it was 3:35. He had burned nearly half an hour making out a shift schedule for Halloween. Stage Harbor was located thirty miles up the coast and it would take him at least forty minutes to get there in afternoon traffic. That would leave him with roughly an hour of daylight to work with. Though the email message had instructed him to come after dark, he would need to see what he was doing in order for his plan to succeed.

Burroughs was a member of the Barnstable County Historical Society. In addition to receiving their quarterly research journal, he regularly attended their presentations and cultural events. He considered himself a well-informed student of local history. This would likely give him an advantage over Abby's captors.

Between 1790 and 1863, some 100,000 slaves were said to have escaped the South via the Underground Railroad. Situated near the abolitionist hotbeds of Boston and New Bedford, Cape Cod's coastal location, and maritime connections made it an important destination within the network. Though there was no formal documentation of the activities that took place, trap doors, tunnels and false walls found in many of the region's oldest structures served to validate the legends passed down by generations of Cape Codders. According to popular myth, the Stage Harbor lighthouse had been a haven for fugitive slaves back in the day.

Built in 1852, the lighthouse stood at the harbor entrance in Chatham. The harbor itself was one of the foggiest points on the east coast and the light had been erected to enhance another beacon already in place. It was situated on a high bluff overlooking Hardings Beach, which was open to the public.

Like many lighthouses in the U.S., the one at Stage Harbor had fallen into private hands. The owner, a supermarket mogul with a passionate interest in all things nautical, had been acquiring lighthouses for years. He owned multiple facilities in various locations, including Fairport Harbor on Lake Erie and Bodie Island in Nags Head, North Carolina. Since the lighthouses were little more than scattered holdings in his vast assortment of private collections, he seldom visited any of them. He was particularly neglectful of the Stage Harbor site, which he had only seen in person once. It remained untenanted throughout the year.

There were at least two remarkable features linking the Stage Harbor complex to the Underground Railroad. A tunnel in the basement of the light keeper's house led to a wooded pathway descending to the beach below. Additionally, the lighthouse itself had a passage beneath the lower service room that was connected to a secluded area outside the compound. Burroughs had toured the grounds with the historical society when it had belonged to the Massachusetts Department of Coastal Management. Though it officially appeared on the national historical register, the site had never been opened to the general public. And so, its intriguing facets were known only to a select group of local inhabitants.

Burroughs doubted that Abby's abductors were privy to that information and he was relatively certain he could locate the entrances to both secret passageways. Getting Abby out safely was another matter entirely. He'd have to improvise. If she was being held in the basement or the lighthouse, there was an outside chance he could rescue her with minimal resistance. But he had no idea about the size of the force he was up against and there was no guarantee that the hidden chambers, unused for well over a hundred years, were still accessible. It was a shaky plan at best. Yet aside from going in with both guns blazing, it was the only one he had at the moment. It would have to do.

He stopped at the front desk on his way out and had a brief conversation with Nadia Welles, who had relieved Annie.

"Are you heading out for the day? She wondered.

"Actually, no. I have some business I have to take care of up in Chatham. I was hoping you could do me a favor while I'm gone."

"Of course, Chief."

"I finished the shift schedule for tomorrow," he said, sliding it across the desk. "Some of the guys have been asking about it. Can you get a hold of everybody who's working and give them their hours? I know I waited until the last minute and I'm sorry. It's been a zoo around here lately."

"Not to worry," Nadia replied affably. "I've got you covered. Do you want me to post the schedule in the conference room after I'm done making calls?"

"Yeah, that'd be great. Thanks."

"No problem. Be safe out there, Chief."

"I will," he said.

As he headed toward the door he thought about the emptiness of that promise.

19

Abby wasn't sure how long she had been blindfolded. After being dragged from her lab and tossed into the trunk of a car, she had lost all perception of time. The ride to her current location could have taken minutes or hours for all she knew. She had been lifted out of the vehicle by a pair of strong hands and roughly escorted down a set of stairs to a musty chamber with a dirt floor. She assumed it was some sort of root cellar. There was no one permanently assigned to guarding her, but she could hear footsteps going up and down the stairs at regular intervals. In the space above, she could make out muffled voices speaking in Arabic. At times, they sounded as if they were arguing. Judging by the amount of activity, she guessed there were at least half a dozen people up there.

Working diligently, she had managed to get the duct tape mostly unstuck from her mouth, making it easier to breathe. Her hands and feet were bound tightly with thick plastic cable ties. She had tried to work them loose, but her efforts were futile. Though she could wriggle about on the floor rather freely, she worried about moving too far from the stairs and provoking the ire of her captors who obviously had no regard for her comfort or safety. She lay quietly on her side, evaluating her predicament.

Her kidnappers appeared to be part of a terrorist group. She wondered if they planned on executing her to enforce some archaic moral code. The man calling himself Michael Kinney had taken pictures with her phone then sent them to Thom's email address. It was an obvious ploy to lure the Chief to her current location. She was confident that he'd come for her at some point and hoped he had the presence of mind to call for backup first. Though her own chances of survival seemed rather slim at the moment, the thought of losing Thom cut even deeper. She wanted so badly to tell him about her feelings for him and desperately hoped she'd get the opportunity.

20

Burroughs took Route 28 into West Chatham then turned onto Ocean Crest Drive which led circuitously uphill to the Stage Harbor lighthouse. Private Property signs warned the public to stay out. The complex was bordered by tall pines that obstructed the roadside view. The path to Hardings Beach was located just below the peak of the hill.

Burroughs hung a sharp right and followed Highpoint Lane to a parking area bordering the public beach. There was only one vehicle in the lot, a late-model Toyota truck packed with fishing gear. Burroughs exited the Jeep and strolled across the tarmac to a set of steep wooden risers leading to the beach below. More than two dozen steps made the descent rather treacherous. The wind coming off the ocean was brisk and caused his eyes to water.

As Burroughs stepped foot on the sand, he encountered a lone fisherman whose hands were full with an assortment of angling equipment. Some of it looked rather cumbersome and the Chief's first inclination was to offer assistance. Unfortunately, there more pressing matters requiring his attention. He gave the fisherman a passing nod and headed up the beach in the direction of the lighthouse.

What remained of Stage Harbor Light was fully visible from a rubble mound breakwater that extended roughly twenty yards into Nantucket Sound. In 1933, an automatic beacon was built on a separate tower and the lighthouse was decommissioned. The lantern room and glass enclosure were removed, though the catwalk and handrails survived. The decapitated structure was directly attached to the light keeper's house—a three-story affair with white clapboard siding. An adjacent storage barn was covered with gray cedar shingles.

Beyond the property, a wooded path provided access from the beach to the lighthouse compound. Burroughs scrambled up a treacherously steep dune onto the trail, stumbling several times and getting sand inside his boots. It grated against his socks as he walked, creating a bothersome distraction.

Though the path was heavily populated with evergreens, scattered birches and oaks had dropped their leaves. They crunched underfoot as Burroughs trudged up the precipitous incline. Tangles of roots beneath the leafy carpet tripped him up every few steps, slowing his progress. As he approached the summit, he scanned the terrain for irregular formations that might indicate the presence of a door or hatchway. He was sure it was around here somewhere and wondered if he had passed it already.

Chipmunks and red squirrels scurried about in the underbrush, busily gathering materials for the coming winter. Some of them chittered irritably at Burroughs for disrupting their foraging activities. A sudden crash in the woods prompted the Chief to draw one of his pistols. He was relieved to discover that the source of the disturbance was a cormorant—a large seabird with a hooked bill and dark plumage. Feeding primarily on fish, they were fairly common to the Cape, though most had departed to warmer climates. Startled into flight, this straggler bolted down the path toward the beach below. Its exodus drew Burroughs' attention to the mound it had been perched upon.

There, embedded in the earth, was a metal porthole.

Holstering his weapon, Burroughs scrambled over to investigate. A covering of moss, leaves, and dirt made the opening virtually imperceptible to any casual observer. Constructed of cast iron, it resembled the entrance to a sewer. He realized that this was the point where his plan was vulnerable to abject failure. If the portal wouldn't open or the tunnel was closed off, he'd have to devise another approach. He could always search for the lighthouse passageway, but it stood to reason that if this one was sealed then the other would likely be as well.

Wasting no time, he grasped the metal ring-pull and gave it an experimental tug. The hatch was wedged securely against its frame and his efforts produced a rasping sound which indicated movement. Encouraged by the results, he repositioned himself and tried again. The thought of Abby bound and gagged gave him a surge of adrenaline. He felt a twinge in his lower back as the door yielded to his exertions, revealing a yawning abyss in the ground below.

Burroughs pulled his flashlight from his pocket and shined it into the opening. A tunnel had been roughly hewn into the earth and reinforced with timber supports. He estimated it to be roughly four feet across and five feet high. Though there were no obvious obstructions as far as the eye could see, he couldn't help thinking about the scurrying rodents and other assorted vermin he might encounter down there. It made his flesh crawl.

Steeling himself against the elements, he sat on the edge of the opening with his legs dangling into the space below. He placed his arms behind him for support then slowly lowered himself into the hole. The air was clammy and stale, leaving a sour taste in his mouth. The dimensions of the tunnel restricted free movement and he was forced to assume a crouched stance to avoid banging his head into the ceiling. He scanned the walls with his flashlight vigilantly as he progressed, keeping an eye out for bats and large spiders. He had been phobic of both since childhood.

The tunnel veered sharply to the left about a dozen paces in. Turning the corner, Burroughs spotted a door at the end of the passageway. Composed of thick wooden planks and hammered metal hinges, it looked like the entrance to a dungeon. He closed the distance quickly and listened for activity in the adjoining chamber. Aside from the insistent pounding of his own pulse, he couldn't hear much of anything.

Burroughs took a deep breath and drew one of his guns, preparing himself for a noisy entrance. He kicked the door with all the strength he could manage and, feeling it give a little, followed with two more solid blows. The last one splintered a portion of the jamb as the door flew open with a resounding crash. His timing couldn't have been better.

Upstairs, the *Asr* prayer was in progress. Scattered about the complex, members of the terrorist cell were kneeling in supplication to Allah. Preceded by an elaborate cleansing ritual, *Wudu*, the late afternoon observance consisted of multiple rounds of silent benediction referred to as *Rakats*. Once the ritual had begun, those engaged in prayer were obligated to continue until the process was complete. This gave Burroughs an unanticipated advantage.

The light was off in the basement, but the door above was slightly ajar, throwing a sliver of light down the stairs. Burroughs noticed that the mortar in the stone foundation was eroded in many spots and the stones themselves had started to shift and bulge. Surveying the chamber with his flashlight, he discovered a human form lying motionlessly on the dirt floor.

It was Abby.

Instinctively, he rushed to her aid.

***

The sudden crash startled Abby. Her first reaction was to find a place to hide, but the blindfold more or less negated that option. She could feel a cool draft coming from somewhere behind her and distinctly heard footsteps approaching. Her body stiffened in anticipation of what might come next. In a shadowy corner of her mind, she imagined that her time had finally expired. This was it! she thought. She'd be yanked roughly to her feet and dragged upstairs, where a camera would record every second of her gruesome execution. The thought of it filled her with dread and despair.

She was surprised when her blindfold was removed by a pair of gentle hands. Her pupils were fully dilated and the sudden exposure to light rendered her temporarily blind. Through a brilliant white haze, she strained to see who was removing her bonds. She felt a wave of elation when Thom's features came into focus. Carefully stripping the duct tape from her mouth, he pressed his lips to hers. Though the kiss was awkwardly timed, it was fervent and sensual. She couldn't remember the last time she had experienced anything so exhilarating. A warm sensation spread from her belly to her extremities as she kissed him back, deeply and passionately. When their lips finally parted, she whispered in his ear.

"I was wondering when you were going to get around to that, Chief."

"I pictured wine and candles, but this will have to do," he said breathlessly.

"It'll do just fine. We can work on the ambiance later."

"Right. We've got to get you out of here. Can you stand up?"

"Yeah," she asserted. "I'm fine ... aside from a few bumps and bruises."

"Do you know how many people are upstairs?"

"I'm not sure. At least six … maybe more."

"I don't like those odds," he remarked soberly. "Time to go."

Abby had no idea how long she had been lying on the floor, but her muscles complained indignantly as she stood with Thom's assistance. Pins and needles coursed through her feet, making it difficult to walk without support. The first few steps were excruciating and she winced in obvious discomfort.

"You okay?" asked Thom with genuine concern.

"Fine," she grunted, "gotta get some circulation going in my feet."

She took another couple of steps and the unbearable tingling began to dissipate.

"Okay, I'm good. So how are we getting out of here?"

Thom directed his flashlight toward the open doorway and tunnel beyond.

"There's a channel through there that leads to the outside. I should warn you that it's a little unpleasant."

"After what I've been through already today, I'm pretty sure I can handle it."

"Good. You're going to want to watch your head. There's not much clearance."

"Got it, thanks. After you, Chief."

She followed him into the passageway, slouching to avoid the low ceiling. She wondered why her captors had not immediately responded to Thom's dramatic arrival and hoped they weren't planning some sort of ambush. Thom moved quickly up ahead, checking behind him every few steps to make sure she was keeping pace. Though her hips and back ached from lying uncomfortably for so long, the rest of her moving parts seemed to be functioning without issue. A sharp right turn brought them to the end of the tunnel. She could see the sky through a metal porthole. It had turned bright orange, indicating the arrival of dusk.

"I'll go first then pull you up," Thom said.

Before Abby had time to raise any objections, he grasped the frame of the porthole with both hands and, bracing his right leg against the wall for leverage, hoisted himself upward. Once he had wriggled through the opening and established solid footing, he extended his arms to her. She held onto them tightly as he lifted her to safety. Her knee scraped against some sharp stones on the way out, tearing a hole in her work pants and scratching her skin. There was a sharp wave of pain that subsided quickly.

"Ouch, sorry about that," Thom apologized. "You okay?"

"It's just a scratch," she told him. "And I've got about a dozen pairs of these pants at home."

"You can send me a bill later," he said jokingly.

Abby thought about kissing him again, but a sudden commotion changed her mind. Cries of alarm were being raised all over the compound. The dialect was unintelligible, but the message was obvious. Someone had discovered she was missing.

Peering through the trees, she could see the doors of a massive storage barn slide open, discharging several men wearing robes and head scarves. They were all armed with assault rifles. She noted that there were two delivery trucks inside the barn, both of them bearing the logo of the rental company they belonged to.

"I'm not sure what's in those trucks," she remarked gravely, "but it can't be good."

"No doubt," Thom agreed. "We need to put some distance between us and this place fast. Follow me."

Angry voices were reverberating in the tunnel as they turned and raced down the wooded path toward the beach. They traveled about fifty yards before the first volley of gunfire erupted behind them. The rounds struck several pine trees to their right, creating a shower of needles and branches that landed harmlessly off the trail. Thom figured as long as they stayed well enough below the shooters and kept moving briskly, they would remain a difficult target to hit.

In spite of the ruddy terrain, they both managed to successfully navigate the entire route without falling once. At the end of the path, a steep dune descended acutely to Hardings Beach. Surveying it from this vantage point, Thom had no idea how he had accessed the trail in the first place. It was three-story drop to the beach below at a ridiculously sheer angle.

"You've got to be kidding me," said Abby, evaluating the perilous decline. "How are we supposed to get down there?"

"We're going to slide," Thom answered, improvising on the fly.

He took off his field jacket and laid it on the ground as Abby stared at him incredulously.

"I hate to be the one to start our first argument as a couple," she said, "but I don't think that's going to work."

"Why not?" Thom countered. "Haven't you ever used one of those plastic sledding sheets?"

"Sure, when I was a kid."

"Well, sand is similar to snow. And my coat's made of Gore-Tex, which is durable and slippery like those sheets. It's the same principle."

"I don't think so," she said doubtfully.

Another volley of gunfire exploded on the trail behind them, missing by a wide margin.

"If we stand here much longer, we'll be literally ducking bullets," Thom asserted. He dragged his coat to the edge of the precipice and sat on it with his legs folded. "People used to do this all the time up in Provincetown before the dunes became a restricted area. C'mon, hop on. It might actually be a little fun."

Abby found Thom's optimism both naïve and persuasive. She settled onto the ground behind him and huddled up close, wrapping her arms around his waist. "This is a helluva way to start a relationship, Chief," she joked.

"Tell me about it," he replied. "Now shift your weight toward the edge along with me."

Their combined efforts sent them hurtling down the slope at breakneck speed. For all the debate it had generated, the ride was over in less than ten seconds. Thom's presumption had been correct. His coat possessed the necessary properties to carry them safely to the bottom, although the landing was rougher than anticipated. They tumbled headlong into the sand together, ending up in a suggestive position with Abby straddling his waist.

"I didn't realize you were such a bad girl," he said mischievously.

"You have no idea how bad I can be," she bantered in a sultry tone.

He felt a pang of excitement in the pit of his stomach.

The tide had receded, leaving a trail of shallow pools in its wake. It was an ideal time for beachcombers. Under different circumstances, Thom might have enjoyed searching those pools for shellfish while taking in the sunset. But a barrage of gunfire in the distance rudely reminded him that this was not the time or place.

"We need to move," he said urgently. "Stay close to the dunes. It'll keep us out of the line of fire."

They untangled themselves from one another and hurried up the beach toward the parking lot, hugging the dunes all the way. By the time they reached the stairs there was no sign of their pursuers and this concerned Thom.

"Let's hope our friends aren't waiting for us up there," he brooded, drawing one of his pistols.

"Do you have another gun I can use?" Abby inquired.

Thom eyed her skeptically.

"Have you ever fired one before?"

"My father was an expert marksman. He used to take me to the shooting range all the time when I was a teenager. I have a Ruger P95 at home."

"Really?" said Thom, taken off guard. "You have a license to carry?"

"Yup. I've had it since I was eighteen."

"You're definitely full of surprises," he commented, pulling the backup piece from his shoulder holster. He would never have let anyone handle it under normal conditions, but given their current predicament, he realized he might need support. "If you've fired a Ruger, then you should have no problem with my Glock," he said, handing her the gun. "It's a department-issued piece and I trust you'll treat it with respect."

"Of course," she promised.

"We'll take the stairs side by side," he instructed. "That way, there'll be two of us returning fire if all hell breaks loose."

"Okay," she agreed, her mouth suddenly feeling very parched.

They exchanged an anxious look, both of them wishing they were someplace safe.

22

Aaban had rarely seen his superior so angry. When news of the escape had disrupted the *Asr* observance, Mullah had summoned both of the men responsible for guarding the hostage to a common area of the house. Though it was written in the Quran that cursing a fellow Muslim was akin to murder, he had shouted hateful things at them. And then, in front of an assembly of witnesses, he had beaten them mercilessly with his judicial cane. The blows had raised ugly welts. Since Mullah was considered a spiritual leader, the men were compelled to endure the punishment without protest. When the regrettable incident was concluded, Aaban approached Mullah inquiring about an immediate course of action.

"We will find the doctor and her accomplice then strike off their heads and fingertips," Mullah fumed, intentionally referencing the Quran.

"And if we don't find them … what then?"

"We must!"

Aaban could see the fury in Mullah's eyes, but felt he would be remised if he failed to defend his position. "With all due respect," he began cautiously, "I believe that we should either stage the event without further delay or postpone it. Our location has been compromised. If we don't act now, we may never get the opportunity."

There was an uncomfortable pause, during which Aaban became convinced he would be the next victim of a brutal caning. But to his complete surprise, Mullah's features softened.

"I'm inclined to agree," the elder said. Quoting the Quran again, he added, "It's time to strike terror into the hearts of the unbelievers. *Allahu Akbar.*"

The Event

1

Thom and Abby were unprepared for what they encountered at the top of the stairs. Though they had anticipated a harrowing confrontation, they found the lot empty aside from a handful of enterprising seagulls. There was no trace of the gunmen in the surrounding dunes and Thom's vehicle sat undisturbed in its parking space. The outcome felt strangely anticlimactic to them both.

"I was expecting a little more excitement," said Abby, lowering her pistol.

"You're right," Thom agreed. "This is way too easy." He holstered his gun and fished the key fob out of his pants, which were now caked with wet sand. The Jeep chirped loudly with the press of a button, scaring the gulls into the air. "C'mon," he said to Abby. "We need to get some place safe and call this in."

"Do you want your piece back?" she offered.

"No. You better hang onto it for now until we're sure there's no one tailing us."

They hopped into his vehicle and sped out of the parking lot in the direction of Route 28, which would take them into West Chatham. They rode without speaking for a little while, still processing the events of the last few hours. There was so much to discuss, neither of them knew exactly where to begin. It was Thom who finally broke the silence.

"So I assume you got a pretty good look at your kidnappers."

"Yeah, the ones who grabbed me from the lab at least. There were two of them," Abby recalled. "One was disguised as a courier. The other was Michael Kinney. I do remember meeting him now. It was after an insurance conference at the clinic a couple of years ago."

"I figured it would come back to you at some point," said Thom.

"For the record, I didn't want to give out your email address, but the guy in the delivery uniform was pretty persuasive."

Thom felt a surge of anger. "Did you see the mask?"

"Yeah. Kinney made a point of showing it to me before I was blindfolded."

"I seriously doubt that Kinney is his real name. I had one of my guys run a background check and there's hardly any information available. He's kept that South Yarmouth address for a couple of years, but there's no trace of him before then."

"That definitely raises a few red flags," Abby remarked. "Did you check out his apartment?"

"Yeah, I found some pretty disturbing material. It looks like he's been planning a major terrorist act. There were maps and pictures and notes. Unfortunately, the notes weren't written in English. I was trying to make sense of them when someone attacked me from behind. I was out cold for a while."

"Are you okay?"

"I've got a pretty big bump on my head, but I'll live."

"I feel terrible," Abby said in a rueful tone. "It seems like I'm always dragging you into trouble."

"Maybe I like trouble," he replied, smiling wanly.

She offered her hand and he took it. The intimacy was reassuring to them both.

Glancing in the rear view mirror, Thom noted that there was no one behind them on the road. He found this unsettling. If the terrorists realized their location had been compromised, why had they abandoned the chase so quickly? "There's a gas station up here a little ways," he said to Abby. "I need to pull over and have a serious talk with Lieutenant Carlson."

2

Carlson knew that Delacroix would pay him a visit at some point, but hadn't expected it so soon. Within a half hour of receiving the financial activity report, the flaky data analyst was standing in his doorway with an arsenal of new information. Delacroix had a tendency to exhibit pressured speech whenever he was excited and Carlson was finding it difficult to absorb all the details.

"I mentioned before that some of the transfers to Randall Landry's account might be linked to organized crime and I found evidence to back it up. I assume you've heard of the Giordano family? The name is synonymous with racketeering. I traced three separate transactions to an offshore account belonging to Carmine Giordano. He's one of the most powerful mob bosses on the East coast."

Delacroix ignored Carlson's invitation to step into the office. He was too engrossed in his rambling discourse.

"I pulled Landry's phone records and discovered that there were over two hundred incoming calls from a man named Carlo De Luca between the first and nineteenth of October. De Luca is on Giordano's payroll, though I'm not sure exactly what he does. Considering the fact that Landry ignored most of his calls, I would say he's some sort of collections agent. Looks like Landry was being harassed and you can bet it had something to do with Giordano's money. I'm still trying to work out exactly what was going on. There's no evidence that Landry was taking any tangible steps toward opening a new medical practice, though he did make a payment to his attorney at the end of September."

Carlson's cell phone began to ring. It was Thom Burroughs calling.

"Maybe Giordano changed his mind about doing business with Landry," Delacroix prattled on. "For all we know, Landry was sleeping with Giordano's wife."

Though Delacroix was providing a host of relevant facts, Carlson hadn't spoken to Burroughs in quite some time and needed to touch base with him. There didn't seem to be any polite way to get Delacroix to stop talking so, at the risk of offending the man, Carlson raised his hands in a 'stop' gesture. "I need to take this," he said firmly.

Delacroix's face assumed a bitter expression as if someone had stuffed a bar of soap in his mouth. He folded his arms primly across his chest then turned and stalked off down the hall. Jesus, thought Carlson, the man is literally pouting. Resigning himself to deal with the fallout later, the lieutenant answered his phone.

"Hey, Chief, what's new?"

"It's good to hear your voice," said Burroughs, sounding slightly out of breath. "I called you a couple of times earlier. I was beginning to wonder if you were dodging me."

"No, I'm just busy as hell. What can I do for you?"

"We need to find a way to close off the Sagamore and Bourne bridges as soon as possible."

Carlson chuckled without mirth. "I'm sorry, did you just ask me to shut down inbound and outbound traffic on the Cape during rush hour?"

"That's right, I did," said Burroughs emphatically. "And if you want to avoid a major incident, you'll make an effort to take me seriously."

"Slow down there, Chief, tell me what's going on."

Burroughs provided a complete recap of his day, including the kidnapping and the visit to the apartment in South Yarmouth where he had discovered the terrorist plans. The scope of the plot was staggering. Thousands of commuters used those bridges every day. In addition to the lives that would be lost during a catastrophic rush hour event, the blow to the infrastructure would be devastating on many levels.

"That's quite a story, Chief," Carlson replied. "If what you say is true, then the evening commute's going to be a real bitch for a lot of people. But we don't have any proof. I can't really call the Department of Homeland Security on a hunch."

"It's more than a hunch," argued Burroughs. "We have DNA evidence linking a notorious terrorist to a murder in Sandwich along with plans to carry out attacks on two major roadways."

"Did you happen to come across any explosives while you were storming the lighthouse?"

"No. But why else would there be delivery trucks in the storage barn? I seriously doubt these guys are organizing a food drive."

"There's no need to be sarcastic, Chief, I believe you," Carlson said. "But I think our story's a little thin for Homeland. They're not going to activate the National Guard without a thorough examination of the facts. Who knows how long that would take?"

"What are you suggesting, we sit back and let these terrorists hatch their plan?"

"No, I'm saying that we'll get a quicker response if we leave the Feds out of it. I'll notify the State Police that there's a looming terror threat on the bridges. They can throw up some roadblocks and search vehicles. I'll send some of my own guys to both locations. Homeland can sort it out later."

"Sounds like a plan," Burroughs said. "The trooper station is right there in the Bourne rotary. And the Sagamore Bridge is just a couple of miles up the Canal."

"So what should we be looking for, aside from guys in turbans screaming 'death to the infidels'?"

"They're using rental trucks with West Virginia license plates. The trucks belong to a company called Appalachia Shipping. There are yellow logos on the doors."

"Okay, that definitely helps."

"They've got about a twenty-minute head start at this point and it'll take the state police a little while to get organized. This is gonna be close, Lieutenant."

"I'm right here at my office in Bourne," said Carlson. "I'll head out to the rotary myself as soon as I call this in."

"What about the lighthouse?" Burroughs pointed out. "There're bound to be a few insurgents still camped out there."

Carlson reacted with a sigh. "Where are you, Chief?"

"I'm at a gas station on Main Street in West Chatham."

"I've got an awful lot on my plate at the moment. Can you handle the situation at the lighthouse?"

"Yeah, there's another trooper station in Yarmouth. I'll try to get a hold of somebody for backup."

"Sounds like a plan. Good luck, Chief. Maybe you and I will find ourselves rehashing this story over a beer someday."

"You never know," said Burroughs, oddly flattered by Carlson's oblique invitation. He didn't even get irritated this time when the lieutenant ended the call without saying goodbye.

3

Thom had used the Jeep's Bluetooth device to contact Carlson, allowing Abby to hear the entire exchange.

"This is crazy," she said after the lieutenant had hung up. "Those trucks are probably halfway to the bridges already."

"Traffic on the major routes gets pretty heavy around Barnstable," Thom pointed out. "It's nothing like the summer commute, but it'll definitely slow them down a little."

"Are we going back to the lighthouse?"

"Well, *I'm* definitely going back. I'm not so sure it's in *your* best interest."

"Why, because I'm a girl?"

"No, because it took me a long time to connect with you and I don't want to lose that."

"I hate to tell you this, but if you wind up getting yourself killed, it'll more or less end our relationship anyway."

"I don't plan on getting killed," he said with conviction. "Not when I'm so close to actually living for a change."

The comment brought a thin smile to Abby's face.

"Right now, I've got a small problem," Thom admitted.

"What's that?"

"I don't have the number to the State Police."

"So use your phone to look it up."

"I don't have the internet on my phone. It's just straight talk," he said, feeling slightly embarrassed.

"That's right," she recalled. "You were ranting about the evils of modern technology just last week. Well, my iPhone got confiscated by a terrorist so I can't help you."

"I'll have to call the station in Sandwich."

"Is your dispatcher's name Siri?"

"Might as well be," he muttered.

Utilizing the voice command feature, he placed a call to Nadia, who was currently running the front desk. She answered on the first ring.

"Sandwich Police Department, how may I help you?"

"Nadia, it's Thom."

"Detective Barber was asking about you. He said you requested some information earlier, then never got back to him."

"Yeah, look, I'm in the middle of something big right now. Can you get me the number for the state police in Yarmouth?"

"Sure. Hang on."

There was a brief pause while she looked it up. He could hear her tapping computer keys. "Are you all right, Chief?" she said worriedly. "You sound a little frazzled."

"I'm fine. I don't have time to get into details. I just need that number."

"Okay, I've got it. Are you ready?"

"Yup, shoot."

He committed the number to memory, offered thanks to Nadia and, without further delay, placed a call to the station in Yarmouth. After about twelve rings or so, it became obvious that no one was going to answer.

"Where the hell are they?" Abby wondered.

"Well, it's rush hour," Thom explained. "I imagine most of the officers are out on patrol. This is Cape Cod, not Boston. There are only so many troopers to go around."

"What about the Chatham police, can you get in touch with them?" Abby suggested.

"Yeah, I could do that, but I know for a fact that they run on a skeleton crew this time of year. Ralph Edwards, the precinct Captain, is a friend of mine. Most days, it's just him and another officer handling calls."

"So what are we going to do?"

"I feel bad about dragging you back out to the lighthouse, but I don't see any way around it unless you want to stay here."

"Not a chance. Don't worry about me. I'm pretty cool under fire."

"This is a serious violation of standard protocol."

"I'm pretty sure protocol went out the window when you handed me your gun."

Unable to think of an appropriate response, Thom just stared at her.

"It's okay," Abby assured him. "I know how to handle myself."

Reluctantly, Thom shifted the Jeep into gear and pulled out of the gas station. He waited until they were about a quarter of a mile up the road before commenting, "You know, you're kinda sexy when you're playing the tough girl role."

"And you're kinda sweet when you're trying to protect me," she replied.

4

Carlson's phone call to the state police in Bourne yielded instant results. All it took was a thumbnail version of the story to motivate the shift supervisor. After issuing an all-points-bulletin with a description of the rental trucks, Sergeant Jim Strack assigned two cruisers to the Bourne rotary and two more to the Sagamore Bridge flyover. He instructed the rest of his units to monitor outbound sections of Routes 28, 6 and 6A. Troopers stationed at the bridges were directed to set up checkpoints with the purpose of searching any suspicious looking vehicles leaving the Cape. Everything was up and running within fifteen minutes.

"Don't worry, we'll get 'em," Strack assured Carlson, "even if we have to back up traffic from Buzzard's Bay to Provincetown."

Carlson assigned a pair of his own men to each bridge then recruited an agent named Derek Thompson to ride along with him. Thompson was one of those lantern-jawed silent types who looked like he should be wearing a lycra suit with a cape. They sat in Carlson's Chevy Yukon outside the trooper barracks, sipping coffee and watching traffic in the rotary. It was crawling along at a glacial pace, a direct result of the roadblock at the foot of the bridge.

Carlson kept up an ongoing dialog with CSI headquarters via his mobile radio unit which he had tuned to a private channel. He was waiting on information about the Appalachia Shipping Company which was apparently located somewhere in West Virginia. Every now and then he pulled out his Android phone and responded to texts from his wife who kept pestering him about having to stay late at work. He was in the process of advising her to eat dinner without him when the radio unit crackled to life.

"Lieutenant, this is Agent Andrews. Over."

Carlson set his phone down and grabbed the speaker mic. "Go ahead, Andrews."

"I've got that information you requested. Over."

"Andrews, you don't have to keep saying *over*, it's actually kind of annoying."

"No problem, boss. Anyway, I have some intel for you. The Appalachia Shipping Company is like a mom and pop version of U-Haul or Penske. They have two locations in Harrisburg County. I was able to get in touch with somebody from the Clarksburg branch. Turns out they rented a pair of trucks to a group of guys last Friday. The manager says he has two valid driver's licenses and a credit card on file. He wouldn't give out names over the phone, but he said they looked like a bunch of Arabs."

"Sounds like our guys," said Carlson.

"Right, well, here's where things get a little scary. I looked into police activity in the area and discovered that there was a major incident at a rock quarry in New Martinsville last weekend. That's less than forty miles from Clarksburg as the crow flies. Somebody made off with a bunch of explosives and there's a security guard still missing. It was a pretty big news story. Apparently, there was enough material stolen to take out half a city block."

"Holy shit," muttered Carlson. This was even bigger than he thought.

5

Thom pulled into the Hardings Beach parking lot and cut the engine. The sun had set and the sky was full of stars. On the hill above them, the tower beacon that had replaced the original lighthouse several decades ago flashed brilliantly, illuminating the harbor at regular intervals. Thom pulled the Glock from his waistband holster and checked the magazine to ensure that it was properly loaded. He instructed Abby to do the same.

"So what's our plan?" she inquired.

"We'll backtrack up High Point Lane onto Ocean Crest Drive toward the lighthouse. It should only take us about five or ten minutes on foot. The road comes out on the western edge of the property where the trees will give us some cover. If we run into trouble on the road, we can scramble into the dunes."

"Do you really think there's anyone still hanging around up there?"

"Well, I know that there are ranks within terrorist cells, just like the military. The lower ranking guys are the suicide bombers. The organizers usually stay behind. But every cell is a little different. I guess we'll find out in a few minutes."

She nodded doggedly, indicating that she was ready to go.

"Abby, in case something bad happens, I just wanted to say—"

She put her hand over his mouth, shushing him. "Don't say anything, Chief. Just kiss me."

Thom put his hands in her hair and gently pulled her towards him. The kiss was slow and soft at first, gaining in intensity as their bodies seemed to melt together. Abby felt a little dizzy when it was over. For a few fleeting seconds, Thom actually forgot why he was there.

6

Bass River, West Dennis
5:35 p.m.

Upon receiving the all-points-bulletin issued by Sergeant Strack of the Bourne unit, Officer Pete Reynolds of the Yarmouth division hopped onto Route 28 and began patrolling his assigned route—a twenty-mile stretch from Chatham to Hyannis. Weather conditions were ideal with dry roads and good visibility. Traffic volume was only moderate. Reynolds listened attentively to his radio unit, hoping for an update of some sort. To his knowledge, there had never been a terrorist threat on Cape Cod, aside from the anthrax hoax in Dennis that had immediately followed the events of 9/11. Though he had received some rudimentary anti-terrorism training at the Plymouth Academy back when he was a green recruit, he felt woefully unprepared to handle the current situation.

After traversing the westbound expanse of his beat uneventfully, he swung into a Cumberland Farms parking lot and set out again in the opposite direction. He was entering Dennisport when one of the rental trucks sped past him in the westbound lane. His stomach executed a full somersault as he grabbed the speaker mic and radioed it in.

"This is Unit 137. All patrols be advised, I have a visual on one of those trucks heading west along Route 28 in Dennisport. I'm in pursuit."

By the time he had activated his flashers and reversed course again, the channel was flooded with chatter.

"Copy that 137. This is Unit 438. I'm in Hyannis and headed east on 28 to intercept. ETA less than ten minutes."

"438, this is 136. I'm in West Dennis. I'm going to set up a checkpoint at the Bass River Bridge."

"Copy 136. I'll be at your twenty shortly."

"This is 137, both positions acknowledged," responded Reynolds.

There were three vehicles between his cruiser and the rental truck, but a few shrill whoops from his siren took care of that problem. The motorists veered onto the shoulder, allowing him to pass. He closed the distance quickly and gave the truck a little tap with his front bumper to assert his presence. The driver refused to yield, accelerating rapidly instead. Reynolds followed suit. Though he realized it would probably be a futile gesture, he switched on the cruiser's loudspeaker.

"Attention," his voice boomed. "This is the Massachusetts State Police. You are resisting arrest. Pull over immediately."

Unaffected, the truck continued toward West Dennis at a rate of nearly seventy miles per hour. Add that to the growing list of infractions, Reynolds thought. When it came time to fill out the paperwork, this was going to be an absolute nightmare.

With two lanes, a narrow shoulder and a variable speed limit, Route 28 was not an ideal venue for outrunning the state police. It didn't take long for the rental truck to get boxed-in by a line of slower moving traffic ahead. Reynolds backed off a bit and maintained a cruising speed of forty-five. When the driver of the truck ignored the turn for Route 134 near the Crocker Neck Marsh in Dennis, Reynolds knew the chase would soon be over. Grand Cove lay just ahead and there were no outlets before the Bass River Bridge where the other units would be waiting. Oblivious to the impending obstruction, the truck maintained its present course.

A lighthouse at the far end of the bridge presided over the entrance to Grand Cove. It was one of few inland lighthouses on the Cape and served very little purpose considering that the clearance of the bridge was insufficient to allow commercial fishing vessels to pass underneath. A network of docks on either side of the overpass housed a wide assortment of small yachts.

What happened next would stick with Reynolds for quite some time. Upon spotting the cruisers stationed at the western end of the bridge, the driver of the rental truck attempted a U-turn at full speed. It was an epic fail. Narrowly avoiding a head-on collision with an oncoming SUV, the truck jumped the sidewalk and smashed through the concrete parapet, plunging into the water below. All three occupants were rendered unconscious on impact. None of them made it out alive. Several hundred pounds of explosives would later be recovered when the vehicle was salvaged from the river bottom.

7

Old King's Highway, Sandwich
5:48 p.m.

Officer Brian Mills was patrolling Route 6 when news of the incident at the Bass River Bridge came in over the radio. A member of the Bourne Division for almost twenty years, he couldn't remember anything quite so unsettling taking place on Cape Cod. Before joining the Massachusetts State Police, he had served in the Army during the Persian Gulf War, completing a full tour of duty. The idea of terrorists in his own backyard infuriated and repulsed him at the same time. He couldn't wait to get a crack at these guys.

Mills followed the Mid-Cape Highway from Barnstable to Exit 2 where he jumped onto Route 130 and headed north toward Sandwich. After passing Shawme Lake, he took a series of side roads that connected him with the Old King's Highway, which was considered by many to be the Cape's most scenic route. A lifelong resident of Brewster, Mills had always enjoyed the quaint homes, colonial style churches and specialty shops that adorned the landscape of this serene tree-lined drive. As he approached Merchant's Road heading east, he spotted a rental truck with a yellow logo on its door. The West Virginia plates were a dead giveaway. He radioed it in.

"All units this is 435. Be advised, I'm on 6A in Sandwich and I just passed one of those trucks heading west toward the Sagamore Bridge. I'm engaging in pursuit."

"Copy 435, this is 442. We're here at the south end of the Sagamore. Traffic's starting to back up onto the Connector. That truck of yours is going to find itself in a serious snarl pretty soon."

"Copy 442."

Mills turned into the parking lot of The Ice Cream Sandwich, which was closed for the season, and jumped back onto 6A with his lights flashing. Navigating around several slower moving commuters, he climbed right up on the truck's tail and held his position. Cars were parked sporadically along the curb so forcing the suspects onto the shoulder was not a viable option. All he could do was escort them toward the massive traffic jam that lay just a couple of miles ahead.

Mills reduced his speed slightly and flipped on his siren. He was preparing to activate the loudspeaker when the back door of the truck suddenly slid open. A gunman dressed in an orange reflective vest unleashed a hail of semi-automatic gunfire. The shots slammed into the front of his cruiser destroying the front grille and taking out one of his tires. He temporarily lost control of the vehicle, careening up over the curb and smashing into a mailbox. Smoke was pouring from under the hood as the cruiser shuddered and stalled right there on the sidewalk.

"Shit," he cursed, pounding the steering wheel with his fist. "This is Unit 435 reporting shots fired," he barked into the speaker mic. "My vehicle's been hit. I'm unable to continue pursuit."

"Copy 435. Do you need medical assistance?"

"Negative, I'm fine. But the suspects are headed your way."

"Acknowledged. We'll be ready when they get here."

***

Aaban gripped the steering wheel firmly and tried to maintain his composure. The officer on their tail was no longer a problem, but a host of additional issues had surfaced. The others had not checked-in at the designated time and were no longer responding to calls on their two-way radio. Fearing the worst, Aaban made a last minute decision. Instead of proceeding to the Sagamore Bridge Connector, where their arrival would be anticipated, he stayed on Route 6A and followed Sandwich Road southwest along the Canal toward Bourne. He was determined to attain at least one objective tonight.

8

Stage Harbor Light, Chatham
5:53 p.m.

Abby and Thom moved stealthily between the pines along the west side of the complex. The caretaker's house was completely dark except for a single light in one of the rooms downstairs. Thom wondered how long the terrorists had occupied the property and how they had managed to avoid detection. Though the house was somewhat secluded, it was noticeable from the harbor below and the tower beacon currently in operation was owned by the Coast Guard. He was sure it was subject to routine maintenance checks.

The storage barn lay just beyond the trees. Both doors were open and there were lights on inside. A long gravel driveway stretched into the blackness beyond the compound. Wary that the crunching of stones underfoot would broadcast their presence to anyone in proximity, Thom stayed on the grass as he approached, motioning for Abby to follow. There was a mullioned window on the side of the building and they crept up to it, peering through the glass.

Two cars were parked inside the barn, a Kia sedan and a Chevy SUV, which had a magnetic sticker on the door bearing the symbol of the Massachusetts DOT. Four men clad in white robes were kneeling on the dirt floor between the vehicles. They were in the process of affixing narrow lengths of PVC pipe to their belts with electrical tape. The sections of pipe, which were aligned in vertical rows, had wires protruding from the ends. Thom had seen pictures of these devices before and knew that they were referred to as "shaheed belts." The word *shaheed* was an Arabic term meaning "holy martyr." It was often applied to suicide bombers.

"Oh my God," whispered Abby. "Are they doing what I think they're doing?"

Thom thought about the plans he had seen in Michael Kinney's apartment. There had been pictures of Nauset Light in Eastham and Highland Light in Truro. Perhaps the terrorists intended to destroy those facilities in addition to the bridges. "There's no negotiating here. We need to take these guys down. Now."

"Won't those explosives go off?"

"I doubt they'd be handling live material. But it wouldn't hurt to exercise a little caution."

Though he was sure the terrorists were armed, he didn't see any rifles in the immediate vicinity. This gave him and Abby a distinct advantage.

"We don't have a clear shot from here," she noted.

"The glass might redirect our bullets anyway. We'll have to go around front."

"Okay," she agreed.

"I'll take the two guys next to the SUV. You take the other two."

Abby nodded her consent. "I haven't used a gun in quite a while," she admitted.

"It's like riding a bike," he assured her. Actually, it wasn't, but he didn't want to sap her confidence. If her shots went wild, he would have to pick up the slack. He felt awful about putting her in this position. Guilt had been eating at him since they had left the gas station in West Chatham. "Are you sure you're comfortable with this?" he asked.

"As far as I'm concerned, it's personal. These guys killed my ex-husband, stole from the clinic and tossed me in the trunk of a car. I think it's time for a little payback, don't you?"

"Definitely," he replied, feeling only slightly better about the situation.

The air had turned crisp and their exhalations produced faint plumes of smoke. A brisk wind was murmuring through the pines. It masked the sound of their footsteps as they crossed the driveway. Thom gestured toward the open door on the left, which would provide the clearest shot. As he and Abby exchanged a final glance, he vowed to spend the next few months wining and dining her if they survived.

Everything happened so fast, Abby could scarcely recall the details afterward. Her first shot hit one of the terrorists between the shoulder blades, leaving a bright crimson stain. He dropped to the ground limply as the man on his right scrambled for cover. Abby's second blast struck the fleeing man's right shoulder. Blood sprayed the driver's side window of the sedan as he howled in pain. The shot had caused some serious damage but hadn't entirely disabled him. He crawled clumsily around the front of the vehicle in pursuit of his weapon, which he would ultimately fail to recover. Thom, who had efficiently eliminated both of his targets by then, rushed over and put an end to the encounter with a carefully placed shot.

Abby had forgotten how deafening guns could be without proper protection. Her ears were ringing so loudly, she could scarcely hear Thom as he spoke to her.

"Are you all right?"

"What?" She practically shouted in response.

"I asked if you were okay," he repeated, raising the volume of his voice.

"I'm fine, I guess. That was the first time I ever shot anyone."

"You and me both. I doubt it ever feels good, even if the person you're shooting at deserves it."

"No kidding," she said morosely.

"I hate to do this to you, but we're not done yet. We need to see if there's anyone in the caretaker's house. There was a light on when we first got here."

Peering over her shoulder, Abby observed that the house was fully immersed in darkness. "Well, it's out now. Somebody must have heard the shots."

"Probably getting ready to make a break for it," he said. "C'mon."

Although the thought of further gunplay filled her with dread, Abby followed Thom out the door into the gloom.

9

Bourne Rotary
5:56 p.m.

Nearly ten minutes had passed since the shootout in Sandwich. The truck had not yet arrived at the Sagamore Bridge and the officers stationed there were starting to get restless.

"This is Unit 442. Does anyone have a visual on that truck? It should have been here by now."

"Negative 442. This is 437, I'm on 6A near the Connector and haven't spotted the suspects yet. They may have bypassed the bridge and headed south. I'm going to check it out."

"Copy 437. Is there anyone else in the vicinity?"

"This is Unit 138, I'm on Route 130 near Forestdale. I'll keep my eyes open."

Carlson was still sitting in his Chevy Yukon outside the trooper barracks in Bourne. He had switched his radio unit to the frequency used by the state police and was listening to all the chatter while working on a package of Freihofer's donuts, which he felt were essential to any stakeout. He had offered one to the stone-faced agent in the passenger seat, but Thomasson or Thompkins or whatever the hell his name was had declined with a dismissive wave of his hand. The man hadn't spoken a word in the last half hour and Carlson was beginning to regret bringing him along. Hell, even a guy like Delacroix would have made better company.

"If you ask me, I'd say they're headed *our* way," Carlson remarked with his mouth full, breaking the monotonous silence.

Agent Thompson merely grunted in response.

Traffic was flowing rather smoothly at the moment despite the checkpoint at the bridge. The 6:00 hour was fast approaching and the volume had begun to taper off. Carlson was about to check his phone for messages when he noticed a white rental truck with yellow stickers entering the rotary via the 6A ramp. It merged with northbound traffic, which was creeping toward the bridge at around ten miles per hour.

"Better buckle up, Captain America," he said to Thompson, "It's time to do battle with evil."

***

Upon spotting the roadblock at the foot of the bridge, Aaban cursed his luck. The mission was now officially in jeopardy. As the man sitting beside him muttered a string of curses, he wracked his brain for alternatives. Though the options were limited, there still might be a way. They could try to circle the rotary and head south on MacArthur Boulevard, maybe hide out for a while down in Woods Hole. Or, they could go ahead and detonate the material short of the bridge. The force of the blast might take out the pilings beneath the approach causing a partial collapse. The casualties would still be significant. Weighing the two choices, Aaban decided that the latter scenario was a more practical option. He waited until they were about twenty yards from the bridge before slowing to a stop.

10

Stage Harbor Light, Chatham
5:59 p.m.

Though it was unoccupied throughout the year, the caretaker's house was fully furnished. Abby and Thom moved from room to room, turning on lights as they did. They were surprised to find the place stylishly decorated with vintage curios and fancy linen drapery. Nautically themed paintings hung from the wainscoted walls. Patterned tiles covered the ceiling. Most of the rooms had fireplaces and sliding pocket doors. A quick search of the first floor yielded no trace of any current inhabitants so they headed up the central stairway, admiring the ornately carved balusters attached to the hand rail. It was a shame that no one actually lived here.

There were four small bedrooms and a bathroom upstairs. A pair of rooms on the east side of the house offered views of the harbor. The other two overlooked the woods. Abby and Thom checked under the beds and in each of the closets, finding them unoccupied. A recessed hatch in the hallway ceiling indicated the presence of a crawl space, but it was too small for an adult to fit through and too high to reach without a ladder. Satisfied there was no one up there, they headed back down the stairs.

Upon reaching the first-floor landing, they heard a door slam in the rear of the house where the kitchen was located. Proceeding directly to the source, they encountered an exit leading to an enclosed breezeway. The breezeway was attached to the lighthouse.

"I always wanted to see the inside of one of those things," Abby said.

"You've never been in a lighthouse?"

"Nope. I was hoping my first one would be free of terrorists."

"There's just no pleasing you," Thom said facetiously.

They stepped through the kitchen door into the breezeway. It was unfinished with exposed joists and chipboard walls. The floor was paved with cobblestones. A metal door resembling a submarine hatch provided access to the lighthouse. It was halfway open, indicating that someone had entered in haste. Footsteps reverberated above, sounding like vibrations inside a metal storage drum. Thom and Abby crossed the threshold with their guns drawn.

Abby quickly located a light switch and flipped it on. The interior was not at all how she had pictured it. Instead of the living quarters she had imagined, it looked more like a boiler room. A massive generator and fuel tank occupied most of the floor space. Electrical conduit and junction boxes covered the cylindrical walls. In the center of the room, a fixed steel ladder led to an opening in the ceiling.

"Most lighthouses have three levels," Thom explained. "The clockworks and what's left of the lantern room are up there."

Thom's brief statement was followed by the roar of a pistol. Two shots fired from the second level slammed into the floor directly in front of him. A third blast struck the ladder and ricocheted wildly about the room. He grabbed Abby and pulled her to the ground, using his body to shield her. Fortunately, neither of them was hit. Recovering quickly, Thom aimed his gun at the ceiling aperture and squeezed the trigger. His shot glanced off the barrel-shaped wall and caromed erratically.

"You better get out of here before this place turns into a shooting gallery," he advised Abby. "I'll chase this guy up onto the catwalk. You should have a clear shot at him from outside. If not, I'll take him down myself."

"Okay," she said, climbing to her feet and planting a warm kiss on his cheek. "Don't get yourself killed, Chief. When this is over, there are a few things I'm going to do to you. I think you'll find them enjoyable."

Thom smiled impishly despite their current predicament. "Oh, I'm sure of it," he replied.

11

Bourne Rotary
6:01 p.m.

Aaban would never know how close he actually came to completing his mission. He was aware that he had been spotted by the troopers stationed at the bridge because he could hear them shouting at him to "freeze" when he exited the cab and approached the roadblock flanked by his two associates. He saw the officers take cover behind their vehicles as Seyed and Hakeem opened fire with their assault rifles. Aaban was so intensely focused on the vast expanse of the four-lane steel bridge that he didn't see Agent Thompson, recently nicknamed "Captain America," enter the scene on foot with a 10mm pistol in hand.

Thompson's first shot struck Aaban in the back of his head, creating a sizeable exit wound on the other side. There was a gout of blood and brain matter as he collapsed to the pavement still clutching the wireless detonator which he had carelessly forgotten to activate. By the time he hit the ground, Thompson had unleashed a volley of shots that left Seyed and Hakeem without significant portions of their skulls.

12

Stage Harbor Light, Chatham
6:03 p.m.

Abby moved quickly through the breezeway and entered the caretaker's house heading toward the front door. Her leg collided with an antique tea table on her way through the living room, scattering fancy china pieces all over the floral carpet. Resisting a compelling urge to pick them up, she continued into the mud room and out the door.

The temperature outside was dropping rapidly. She could see frost beginning to form on the ground. The brittle air burned her lungs a little as she raced around back toward the lighthouse. A pale glow was emanating from the louvered exhaust vents situated on either side of the lower service room. The rest of the structure was a blackened silhouette against the skyline. She circled the perimeter with her gun pointed at the catwalk, trying to find the clearest shot. She ended up near the bluff overlooking the harbor. Waves were pounding the beach below and the roar of the surf was strangely hypnotic. Staring expectantly at the circular platform high above her, she waited for an opportunity to end this tiresome ordeal once and for all.

She didn't have to wait long.

A sudden exchange of gunfire erupted inside the lighthouse, the reports muffled by the incoming tide. Seconds later, a hatch in the center of the catwalk opened like the lid of a soup can. A diffuse pillar of light radiated into the night sky, temporarily eclipsed by a figure emerging from the space below. Abby recognized the man immediately and opened fire, emptying her magazine. Several errant shots pinged off the hand rails ineffectually, creating sparks. But a number of rounds struck Abdullah Rashid's body, tearing apart organs and rupturing major arteries.

"Die, you son of a bitch," Abby muttered as the terrorist's flaccid corpse tumbled over the railing and plummeted three stories to the unyielding earth below. Her own body went numb for a few seconds before the horrific events of the past few hours came flooding back to her all at once. She slumped to the ground with tears streaming down her face, feeling exhausted and overwhelmed. As Thom rushed out of the lighthouse to comfort her, she knew there'd be better days ahead.

Epilogue

Two days later, Burroughs and Carlson met at Bobby Byrne's Pub in Sandwich. It was an eclectic food chain with other locations in Hyannis and Mashpee. Burroughs had habitually avoided the place out of loyalty to his friend Paul McLeod who claimed that Byrne, a real person, had been stealing ideas from other restaurants for years. Though Burroughs found the menu relatively uninspiring, the atmosphere was friendly and the beer list extensive. He sidled up to the bar and ordered himself a draught of O'Hara's Irish Stout. He was curious to see how Carlson would behave outside the confines of his job.

There weren't many surprises. The lieutenant showed up a half hour late dressed in his customary collared shirt and tie. He offered no formal greeting as he deposited himself on the stool next to Burroughs. He was rather gruff about flagging down the bartender, an attractive blonde in a tight-fitting pencil skirt. After he had caught the woman's attention, he asked Burroughs what he was drinking and then ordered a Coors Light for himself. "Is the food any good here?" He offered as a conversation starter.

"I don't know," Burroughs replied. "I've driven by the place a million times, but never actually stopped in. A friend of mine owns the Laughing Gull Pub in Dennis. I feel sort of guilty being here … like I'm cheating on him or something."

Carlson nodded blankly, content to move on to other topics. "So I imagine you're still wondering about the case. I can fill you in if you're interested."

Actually, Burroughs hadn't thought much about it at all over the past twenty-four hours. He had spent a majority of that time in bed with Abby, napping and snacking between passionate bouts of lovemaking. "I'm definitely interested," he responded courteously, channeling his thoughts back to less pleasant matters.

Over the next twenty minutes or so, Burroughs listened attentively as Carlson covered a wide range of topics from Abdullah Rashid's complete facial reconstruction to Randall Landry's grand business plan.

Carlson explained how Randall's failure to secure a loan by conventional means had driven him to consort with less reputable investors. This set off a chain of events that led to his murder. The money invested by mob boss Carmine Giordano had come with strings attached. Landry had agreed to perform a breast augmentation procedure on Giordano's wife Claudia, an Italian-American beauty who was half Giordano's age. Showing an almost depraved lack of restraint, Landry had seduced her. Upon finding out, Giordano had threatened to have Landry "whacked" and assigned one of his goons to get his investment back. Since it represented more than half of what he had accrued to that point, Landry sought alternative ways to recoup the funds. He approached his father at one point, spinning a tall tale about being blackmailed by his ex-wife. Douglas Landry was fairly straight-laced and would never have approved of Randall's choice of business partners. Hence, the fabricated story.

Carlson paused to drain the rest of his beer, which he claimed was warm and flat. He didn't immediately order another one and Burroughs took this as a cue that he was preparing to leave. There were still a few missing pieces of the puzzle, though.

"I guess I still don't understand what prompted Rashid to kill both Landrys," Burroughs said.

"Well, the details are a little sketchy," Carlson began, "but we assume Randall threatened to go public with Rashid's identity if he didn't submit to the doctor's monetary demands. Reconstructive surgery doesn't come cheap and Rashid had paid in cash so Randall knew the guy was loaded. Since Douglas had assisted with Rashid's surgery, he represented another loose end. It turns out that Rashid was aligned with the ISIS terror group. We're not sure if Randall knew this or how he was able to locate Rashid after so much time had passed. What we do know is that Randall ended up being murdered by one sociopath while trying to save himself from another."

There was an extended pause while Burroughs swigged the rest of his beer and Carlson fished in his wallet for tip money. It had become obvious to both men that they had very little in common outside of work. Carlson tossed a couple of bucks on the bar and stuffed his wallet back into the side pocket of his cargo pants.

"I wasn't sure what to make of you at first, but you ended up being a real help to us," the lieutenant said sincerely. "Without you, those terrorists might have carried out their plans. I owe you a debt of gratitude. Hell, the whole state of Massachusetts owes you."

It was the nicest thing that Carlson had ever said to him and Burroughs was left temporarily speechless. He shook Carlson's outstretched hand and smiled mutely.

"If you're ever looking for a job with the state CSI unit, give me a call. I'd hire you in a heartbeat," Carlson added. Having said a mouthful, he abruptly walked out of the restaurant.

Burroughs watched him go, wondering if their paths would ever cross again. He certainly hoped not. If he completed the remainder of his career without another high-profile murder case or terror threat, it would suit him just fine.

The bartender removed Carlson's glass from the bar and picked up Burroughs' empty stein. She leaned in close and batted her pretty blue eyes at him, suggesting that she might be interested. Burroughs estimated her to be somewhere in her late thirties or early forties.

"So, your buddy left you all alone, eh? Do you need a refill?"

"He's not my buddy," Burroughs replied. "He's just someone I ended up crossing paths with at work."

"Oh, what do you do?"

"I'm the Chief of Police here in Sandwich."

"That sounds exciting," she replied, looking genuinely interested.

"Sometimes it is," he told her, "Especially lately."

"You working on something big right now?"

"You could say that. But it doesn't have anything to do with my job."

"Let me guess," she said, "you just started a new relationship."

"Hey, you're pretty good at this."

"When you talk to as many people as I do, you develop ESP."

"It's not really a new relationship," Burroughs offered, surprised to find himself opening up to a stranger. "I've known her for a long time."

"Well, that's even better," she commented. "You guys have a history to build upon."

"Yeah," he smiled. "She's definitely the best thing that's happened to me in the past few years." Reaching into his coat pocket, he pulled out a velour ring box and placed it on the bar. Again, it was unlike him to be so unguarded around people he hardly knew. Maybe it wasn't such a bad thing.

"Is that what I think it is?" the bartender asked.

"It's not a ring," he told her. "I don't think we're quite at that point yet. It's the key to my house."

"Well, that's another very big step," she said, inspecting the contents of the box. "You going to give this to her tonight?"

"I was hoping to, yeah. I guess I'm a little nervous."

"About what?"

"I don't know, rejection I suppose. It's been a long time since I've done this."

"Are you having doubts about the relationship?"

"Not at all," he said confidently. "I've never been so sure about anything."

"Then you should definitely follow through," she advised him. "Chances left untaken are the ones we most regret."

It sounded like wise counsel to Burroughs. "My name's Thom," he said, extending his hand. She shook it.

"I'm Helen," she offered, smiling warmly. "I feel like I should call you Chief for some reason. I like the way it sounds."

"Yeah, a lot of people call me that. I like it, too."

"Well, it's nice to meet you, Chief. Are you ready for another round?"

He mulled it over for a few seconds, imagining the rich flavor of O'Hara's mingled with the complex aroma of coffee and licorice. Burroughs was a connoisseur of beers and had yet to sample a better one. But Abby was waiting for him at home and he was anxious to get back to her.

"No, I'll pass," he said, picking up the ring box and returning it to his coat pocket. He slipped a five dollar bill onto the bar as a tip. "It was nice talking to you, though. I really appreciate the advice."

"No problem. Stop in again sometime," she said.

"Maybe I will," he said, wondering what his good friend Paul McLeod would have to say about that.

All the way home he thought about the untaken chances that had characterized his personal life over the past several years. There was very little to be gained without risk. He realized that now and he was confident about taking the next big step with Abby. It was time to put all the old, painful memories to sleep. If the boneyard wind came calling again, he'd be in a much better place. He would be ready to resist it.

Afterward

Though most of the places in this novel are very real, some of the details have been fabricated or exaggerated for dramatic effect. For the sake of literary convenience, liberties have been taken with the layout of various towns and roadways as well. However, the tranquil beauty of Cape Cod has not been exaggerated in the least. If my father were alive today, he would strongly urge anyone who has never been there to start making travel plans. The Cape Cod Chamber of Commerce is a good place to start. You can find them on the web at: capecodchamber.org.

~Jonathan Weeks

About the Author

For over thirty years, Don Weeks was among the most popular radio personalities in the Capital District region of New York State. He received a Marconi Award for radio excellence in 2005 and was inducted into to the New York State Broadcasters Hall of Fame four years later. He had just completed a rough draft of Scarecrow on the Marsh when he died of Merkle Cell Cancer in March of 2015. Author royalties from this project will be donated to the WGY Christmas Wish Campaign. Weeks worked tirelessly over the years to help raise money for the charity.